THE PILLOWS

BY THE SAME AUTHOR:

THE PILLOWS

BY BENNY ANDERSEN

TRANSLATORS: BENNY ANDERSEN, CYNTHIA ANDERSEN,
NADIA CHRISTENSEN, JUDITH DOYLE, LEONIE MARX,
ALEXANDER TAYLOR, AND DONALD WATKINS.

Curbstone Press
321 Jackson Street
Willimantic, CT 06226

Borgens Forlag
Valbygårdsvej 33
Copenhagen

A Note on the Translation: Three of the stories in this volume, »Layer Cake«, translated by Nadia Christensen, »Hiccups«, translated by Leonie Marx, and »The Pants«, translated by Donald Watkins, first appeared in *Selected Stories* (Curbstone Press, 1983). The remaining stories were jointly translated by Benny Andersen, Cynthia Andersen, Judith Doyle, and Alexander Taylor. All of the translations have been checked by the author and several of the translators.

The Pillows (Puderne) was originally published by Borgens Forlag (Copenhagen) in 1965.

This book has been published with the support of:

The Augustinus Foundation
The Connecticut Commission on the Arts
The Danish Government Committee for the Promotion of Literature Abroad

Danish ISBN 87-418-5580-9

U.S. ISBN

LC

Contents

I

The Break

There was something particularly confidence-inspiring about his tiny mustache, which gently sloped out over his mouth, a little thatched smile. He liked to begin by relating an experience he'd had on the way over here, whatever the weather, he'd experienced something. One day when it was pouring he'd seen an old fogey with a skipper's cap and cycle clips carefully washing a telephone booth with swab and dough scraper while the water splashed down on him and made the pail overflow. One sunny day he'd seen an older lady cross some hopscotch squares, stop, look around, hop two squares and lose her balance in the third, then hurry on. It was as if things waited to happen until the moment he came by, people got run over just as he was opposite them, big dogs immediately began coupling with very small ones, and he talked about it so that I saw it before my eyes and wanted to shout: Please take me with you sometime, let me walk beside you when something like that happens, and be sure to tell me when it happens! – – because I never seem to experience anything exceptional.

But gradually he would get quiet and introspective. I became exasperated by this prelude and tried my best to bring life into his eyes again, asked him anything that occurred to me, some of the burning issues of the times: What do you think about all the big strikes right now?

He turned toward me again. His smile became smaller and his mustache contracted like a little hedgehog.

»Oh, well . . .« was all he said. That was enough. He must have experienced some inconceivable upheavals or had to have enormous inner strength when things that made everyone else bite their nails or beat their breasts and rage were for him worth only a slight grimace. Later I tried to imitate it at the office when there were stormy discussions about current problems, but I'm afraid nobody noticed and hurried on with the lively discussion as if I hadn't immediately made any further discussion unnecessary −− either because I lacked the tiny effective mustache or because I was the youngest man in the office. But I had to hurry on with a new question before he withdrew into himself again.

»If I could afford it, I wouldn't mind going to France for my summer vacation. It should be very interesting.«

Again he sniffed his mustache up a little, this time his eyes grew almost melancholy, he nodded slightly and mumbled: »Well, maybe . . .«

I could have told myself that. Clearly he meant if I wanted to go, then maybe it wasn't the most boring place to go, even though there were, of course, much more profitable regions on the globe. I couldn't afford it anyway, so why didn't I say Africa or Tierra del Fuego? In any case, one thing was clear to me: I would never set foot in France.

He used to tutor me in geometry because I wanted to be an engineer. I gave up on it because I never got a solid foothold on the subject. It might have been partly his fault since he clearly didn't care for the subject and talked about everything else imaginable, and so it became boring for me, too. But it was lucky that it was he rather than some consummate geometer who took me under his wing. Maybe then I'd have believed even today that that's the focus I should concentrate on and never have experienced the burning desire within me for something I couldn't define but which I was convinced he could explain to me when he felt I was ready. And even though the constant delay was about to drive me crazy, and even though things went as they did, I wouldn't have missed that feeling for all the circles, parallelograms and bridgebuilding projects in the world.

Later he kept on coming to see us whenever he gave lessons in the neighborhood, he knocked about the city as a tutor, it was this public existence that seemed to suit him best. So he dropped by and sat down, barely unbuttoned his thin blue-gray jacket, the same one summer and winter, and chatted with me and my mother. She idolized him, but since I felt he couldn't speak plainly to me about his plans while she was in the room, I often asked her to leave us alone when she had brought in the coffee. When he had left she came in and, interested, asked how we'd progressed and so she shouldn't find it odd that we hadn't gotten any further, I told her we were making progress, that we were on the verge of figuring something out together, but it had to be prepared for from the start, it was a question of the approach.

He must have had something in mind, coming to visit me as he did. He usually had a record with him I should borrow, or a book. One time he lent me a Mozart symphony, no, he entrusted it to me with a confidential air, as if this very record was the secret source he drew on, which gave him his special and unshakeable view of every phenomenon, and now at last the time had come for him to initiate me into his secret. As soon as he'd gone, I put the record on, my heart hammering with exitement, and at the very first sparkling measures I cried with relief, for this was it, I sat in the midst of the web of tones in the enchanted spot I had dreamed of.

The next time he came I stumbled over my words trying to explain my happiness to him. I'd played the record a few dozen times before my mother felt that that was enough. He nodded in a friendly and thoughtful way, but I could see at once that that wasn't all. Then he took out a small tattered book and handed it to me, and when I was alone I immersed myself in Dostoevsky's book about the underground man, who wouldn't lick his sores, but kept them open, gnawed them larger, ate himself in order to put an end to his suffering, this was the bottom, the underground dark, and the gnashing of teeth beneath Mozart's light-filled halls. How right of my friend to make me aware of this side of existence. Not until now had I seen how immense and self-contradictory life was, and I was better prepared to meet it than ever before. I didn't dare say it right out to him, but the time must have come when he'd show me the way. But he simply nodded and smiled wryly. I was dumbfounded, I couldn't conceive of anything being truer than this, but he came with work after work, book after book. Each time it was as if he took back what he'd shown me as if it weren't good enough for me after all; there had to be tougher things encountered before I could gain full insight.

What did he want with me? I had to believe that he had special plans, and I thirsted to know them and to carry them out, reach the promised land he could get the passport to, but here we sat month after month in the same place, on the same two chairs, opposite each other, he with his overcoat on, I without one. I began to sleep poorly at night, had no appetite at mealtimes, became irritable — — one day my mother reproached me for not taking the garbage out for a week so that she had to divide the surplus trash between diverse cartons and cracker tins, I hurled the book I was reading at her. At the office I couldn't concentrate on my work anymore, my job was something purely temporary, a tuft in the middle of the stream from which I'd take off in my leap over to the bank of salvation once it emerged from the fog, and naturally I had to devote my time to watching for the bank and not tending to the tuft.

12

Nothing interested me. I never went to the movies, didn't leave the house, stopped seeing my girl because she reminded me too much of everything here and now, this vicinity, made me fed up with it, spring which let things happen and buds blossom, but not for me, all the little inclinations and habits which had marked off my existence until now, but which I was ready to deny the moment he snapped his fingers and said: »It's time to go!« Finally she and I couldn't talk together anymore, since I couldn't endure using common words and phrases, and new ones hadn't yet arrived, conversation stopped, and the relationship gradually ebbed out. One day my hasty work and drawer-reading got to be too much for my boss. He gave me a serious warning, and I jumped up and gave him my resignation on the spot.

My mother was appalled and angry. I had to calm her down by saying I had another excellent prospect.

»You don't mean, do you, anything to do with what you've chewed on for two years now without profit?«

»Great undertakings demand extra long preparations,« I said, »but the time has come. You must be extra friendly tonight, he usually comes Wednesday evening. Buy something nice to go with the coffee.«

»As if I'm not always friendly when he comes.«

»But extra friendly, you must be so friendly as not to come into the room at all.«

I had straightened everything up, as usual filled the sofa with thick pillows, had a pack of cigarettes and a box of cheroots lying out even though he didn't smoke. But what if he got the urge to someday, maybe it would be me who'd light his first cigarette or cheroot, I was curious to know which of them he'd prefer, and since it was improbable that he'd begin to smoke cigarettes and cheroots at the same time, it meant that one of the packs was bought in vain, since

13

neither I nor my mother smoked. However, I took it very cold-bloodedly, whereas the thought that he might suddenly get the desire to smoke a pipe sent cold shivers down my back. Or maybe he wouldn't like that particular brand of cheroots, he would want a longer one, or a cigar – – to be really safe I should have a tobacco shop, so I hoped deep down that he'd refrain from tobacco, even though that meant that both the cigarettes and cheroots were bought in vain. There are certain things to which one can't apply utilitarian views.

At our harbors and canals hang certain rescue gear, for example, which can be useful in a dangerous situation, but for which you hope there will be no need whatsoever.

Sure enough, he came out in the afternoon, sat in his usual chair and unbuttoned his jacket without taking it off. The sun shone directly in on him so that he grimaced, and now I saw that he'd lost weight in the course of the winter, he looked so tired and pale, even his moustache was faded, and his smile lines had added new offshoots.

I slapped a few of the pillows so they looked extra nice and puffed out, but he remained sitting in the chair, shading his eyes with his hand, so I went over and drew the curtains until his face came into shadow.

»I've come to say goodbye,« he said. »I've had enough of life here in the city, so I'm going back to my hometown to regain my strength.«

My heart began to pound. Of course, I should have thought of that: his birthplace had to be where all the conflicting truths he'd taught me were gathered into one.

»I'm ready to leave at any time.«

He took his hand from his eyes and looked attentively at me.

»What do you mean by that?«

I got up – – »I'm ready to go with you!«

He gazed at me. Then he shook his head with a melancholy smile.

»That's out of the question. What good would it do? And you have your job to take care of here.«

»No,« I triumphed, »I just quit today!«

Then he creased his forehead and scratched his moustache.

»Well, that's your own affair,« he said. »Anyway, I have to travel alone. I need to be by myself.«

Everything went black. I turned and went over to the window so he wouldn't see my despondency.

»When are you coming back?« I asked.

»You'd better prepare yourself for the fact that I'm not coming back. I've come to say goodbye for good.«

I took hold of the windowsill, I clung fast to the notion that he hadn't said »I'm never coming back,« but on the contrary, »you'd better prepare yourself...« – – my patience should be trained to prepare indefinitely, it could be months or years, but how long would I be able to cope alone?

I pulled the curtains open again to get a good look at his face, but he took his hand from his eyes and got up.

»Thanks for the pleasant time together and all the good chats.«

He added insult to injury by reducing our meetings, which were so full of perspectives on the future and secret understandings, to pleasant times together – – I was stunned. I showed him out and remained standing at the door, listened to his steps down the stairs.

»Has he gone already?« My mother came out from the kitchen. »And I've just made the coffee.«

»Keep it warm until I get back,« I said. Then I hurried in for the cigarettes and cheroots and ran down the stairs.

As long as I kept close to the wall a few houses behind

him, there was no great danger that he'd see me. He went in the direction of the harbor so that soon we came down into the long coal street behind the quays. The whole area is a coalmountain landscape with the narrow silos towering up here and there and crane stagings with the stiffened cranes which are also coal-black against the red evening sky. Along the coal street ran long billboards where the names of the companies were painted with meter-high dirty-white letters, each name measuring nearly half a kilometer. *The Danish* you read, and that takes about five minutes, and then you know that a dull sequence is coming because all the dull Danish companies begin with The Danish or The United, and sure enough, ten minutes later you've wandered through the dullest of all company names: The Danish Coal Company, and you're relieved that it's over, and then a little later there comes like an uncontrolled yawn the letters: INC into the bargain. Anyway the street interested me at that moment for one reason: he walked in it, all the while I thought: What is he feeling walking here, what is he getting out of these desolate billboards and deserted coal-heaps, what couldn't he say about them? The only living creatures at this time were two dogs who coupled between the rails of a dumpcar, I saw him shoot a short glance at them but I was convinced that he'd seen something interesting about them and was ready to tell about it in a pinch. I hurried over and tried to imagine what he'd seen, but I saw nothing more than two dogs coupling and since they were exactly the same size, I'd have no idea what I should fasten upon if anyone had asked.

When I got out onto the quay he'd vanished from my sight. On one side were two freighters, it could be he had gone on board one of them, but they looked so deserted that I walked toward some small houses at the end of the quay, one of them had red and green beer signs between

16

the windows, a dive. I peeked in over the half-curtains, and there he sat in a corner by himself drinking beer.

I felt to see if I had any money on me and went in. Husky voices, sour tobacco juice and the crackling of dice closed in over me. It was the first time I'd been in a place like that. I sat down by the entrance and ordered a beer. He looked up a moment as I sat down, but concentrated again on his glass. I boiled with vexation and confusion and nearly knocked over my glass when I went to fill it. Some card players looked over at me and said something in a low voice to each other before they went on loudly playing.

The beer was ice-cold, but felt hot and peppery in my stomach, little by little the warmth oozed out into my limbs, into my skin, into my head, it was as if a pair of corks had been taken out of my ears, the voices, the sound of glasses and the dice and the smack of cards cut into my head, I could hear everything that was said, even at the farthest table.

I got another beer, this time I held the glass firmly, but the neck of the bottle rattled against the glass so much that the card players scowled at me again, and this time I caught the words: A whelp like that shouldn't be allowed . . .

I got up and went over to my friend.

»Hi,« I said, »Won't you say hello?«

My own voice rang loud and strident in my ears. Perhaps I really spoke as loudly as that, but I couldn't speak any lower. He unwillingly looked up at me.

»Go on home. We've said goodbye to each other.«

»That's not the way we play the game,« I said. This time I didn't try to speak softly.

One of the card players got up.

»Is he bothering you, mister?«

My friend shook his head.

»I don't think so,« he smiled.

»Otherwise just give a call. But perhaps you know him?«

My friend tightened his moustache in the manner I knew so well.

»No, I don't know him.«

I threw myself across the table so that his glass tipped over.

»That's a lie,« I shouted, »the damndest lie, he knows me very well, we're – –«

»That's it!« – – A huge fist took me by the shoulder and swung me round. I saw a fat red face in front of me and struck out at it with all my might, but my hand never reached its target, my arm was wrenched behind my back and I was tossed out.

»Faggot!« rang out after me as the door was yanked shut.

I hid behind a stack of fish crates and waited at least an hour. At last he came out, looked all around, and hurried along the quay.

I followed and came up alongside him.

»Good evening,« I said, »tell me, don't we know one another?«

It was fairly dark and overcast, but the lights on the quay hadn't come on yet. He quickened his pace and looked nervously at me.

»What are you up to?« he asked.

»I'll stick to you like a bur,« I said and began to laugh, bur, I didn't know where I got that from, but it was really a funny word. I felt good now, in my body, I mean, light and luke-warm, there was just something I had to get straight with him, that lay like a little sharp object in my head and bothered me every once in a while, but there was no hurry about examining it more closely, we could talk a little first.

»What are you really feeling walking here,« I asked in a friendly way.

»Feel something yourself,« he said, irritated and out of

breath, he walked quickly now, he had shorter legs than me. »You can't rely on me forever. Find out about things for yourself.«

Then he began running down the quay and I bolted after him without wanting to plague him, I just wanted to go along. Not until he was about to stumble over a mooring did my head suddenly become so full of these sharp objects that I was about to scream. In one leap I was next to him and gave him a push out over the edge.

I stared down after him, at first I thought he'd gone to the bottom, but shortly after I heard a splash farther out, he'd popped up in an entirely different place and swam away from shore with long, dogged strokes.

I rummaged in my pocket and got hold of the cigarettes.

»Cigarettes?« I shouted and threw them at him.

»Or cheroots?« I let the cheroots follow, but he was too far out. It was dark now, and since I couldn't see him anymore, I sat down on a bollard and dozed away. I don't know how long I sat there, but I was shaking with cold when I woke. The lights were on.

Now I got terrified by what I had done, I didn't grasp that it was me who'd pushed him in – – had he drowned?

Then I noticed the lights from the other side of the harbor. Naturally he'd swum over there. I began to run around the basin, I should be able to find his footprints, wet as he was. I had no idea of what I'd say to him, ask for forgiveness, perhaps, I just ran.

I found the place where he pulled himself out and stooping followed the drops in between some warehouses. Then it began to rain. I ran a little further in their direction before the raindrops flowed together too much, but when I came to an intersection the asphalt was completely wet and shone brightly in the glare of lights. The trail could lead anywhere. I turned homeward.

»Where have you been, I've stayed up half the night keeping the coffee warm,« my mother scolded.

»Let me have a cup, then.«

»I've drunk it all now,« she said bitterly. »I'll see if there's more. Any luck, did you find him?«

»No.«

»What about your plans and your beautiful new job?«

She put a half run of dregs in front of me.

»I'll have to figure something out myself.«

The Extension Phone

That morning I had forgotten my bow tie as usual, so I had to dash across the street to the department store and buy a new one. The reason is that I go to night school and can't get up in the morning − − usually my mother manages to get my lunch bag tossed down the stairs after me, but the bow tie she never thinks of. Fortunately, there are some cheap ones over in the department store. They're crude looking and probably made from some curtain material that's gone out of style or something, flowers and dots, I've gradually accumulated a score or more of them at home, so that if I ever have to choose material for curtains, I'll just take them along with me and say: Anyway, it shouldn't be any of this kind of stuff. Naturally it would be smart to have a dozen of them lying in a drawer in the office, but that's the kind of thing you never give a thought to in the morning. My mother, by the way, has experimented with different systems for waking me, for a while she slapped ice-cold washcloths over my face, but you get accustomed to that quickly. Then she thought of placing a cup of hot coffee in my hand while I was lying down. So it was a question of balancing myself up on my elbow without spilling it. I still fell back asleep again, the first two times with the result that the cup tumbled out of my hand and I scalded my arm and Mother swore about the bedclothes, but it was her own idea, after all. Other than that it worked for a while, but it's amazing how quickly you learn to sit up on your elbow and sleep like a log with a cup of scalding coffee in your hand without spilling a drop, so she's probably devising a new system now, maybe something with sneezing powder or fire-

21

crackers. The people over in the department store got to know me, the clerk with the receding hairline suddenly scoops down into the box with bow ties and lets them drip from both hands as if it were a treasure chest he were showing. He probably thinks I'm awfully vain. The truth is I don't think the people in the office notice whether I've a bow tie on or not. It's simply a question of honor for me. I'd really rather wear a regular necktie, but that would be far too expensive with my rate of consumption.

Well, then I go back to the office, and in addition to the morning mail there's a square brown package lying on the counter. The mail and packages are my domain. I'm the one who takes care of the phone, too, both jobs are rather important when you really think about it. For a while there was a hitch with the telephone, it was around exam time for my course last spring. I'd gotten a case of nerves and be-gan to stutter and it didn't sound too good when I answered the phone and started to say Ga-ga-ga-ga and a quarter hour later Garborg & Company. So Toft took over that job for a while until the exams had been passed.

The package was for the head clerk so I went in to him with it.

»Aha,« he said. »It's my extension phone. They're coming at noontime to set it up.«

When I came back into the outer office and sat down to sort the morning mail across from Toft, he whispered:

»What's this, is he going to have an extension phone now?«

Toft is a strange sort. He's big and flabby and no doubt very funny, but since I'm usually the one he makes fun of, I don't care much for it. I mean, to take it out on someone younger, it's like teachers and that sort, no, by god, it's too easy. Like, for example, when he tries to make me stutter, he obviously can't remember the time that he had to take

22

care of the telephone. Even if, calm and poised, I say holi-
day mail, he begins immediately: hawl-hawl-hawl, what
kind of a hall are you talking about? and ripples with laughter as if I had really stuttered, and if I don't immediately
join him in his laughter, preferably a little selfconsciously,
he gets very superior and begins to find mistakes in some
invoices I have written or sends me out to buy some cheroots or something else silly. I think that's a weakness in a
grown person. I've written that down in the little blue book,
too, where I keep that kind of thing. Among other things
I've written: Never take advantage of an inferior's defenselessness, even if it amuses you at the moment. – – Perhaps
it's not expressed so well, but I'm the only one who will use
it, so I can always correct it. There are lots of other things in
there, too, but most of it deals with how I don't want to be.
Maybe I'll find out later how I would like to be, for the moment I'll have to get along with this. Oh, yes, there is one
single thing, by the way, but I'm a little sorry about it now
because it was something the head clerk had said, and he is
far from being a model for me, but I thought it was fair to
write it down. He said one day: It isn't so much the result
that counts as good intentions. Now that I think it over, I
think it's pure nonsense, because if I've ever had anything,
it's been good intentions, both in putting the index cards in
their proper order and in saying Garborg & Company without stuttering, but by God it's the mistakes they get all worked up about, all the correct things they simply take for
granted without acknowledging them. Someday I'll cross it
out when I find something better. But it really sounds very
good.

In all fairness I have to say that of all things, boring Toft
is not. He is entertaining in a way that doesn't make the
work suffer, so you don't need to sit with pursed lips in the
middle of a joke when the boss walks through on a rare oc-

23

casion. He makes the most boring work fun. So I sat watching to see whether he would think up something crazy with the extension phone, but it came in an entirely different way than I had thought.

First he sat looking out the window as usual, it takes a while before he gets going in the morning. He said one time: »I can't start on anything before my soul gets here, it didn't catch the trolley.« I've written that down, too, but I've put a question mark beside it because it reminds me of something or other I've read someplace. Otherwise it sounded good. But today that wasn't what was wrong. Suddenly he looked over at me and said:

»You're really a very sensible chap, Henrik, I'd like to ask you a question. Suppose that we had a mirror sitting here between us just under the coca-cola calendar — — so we could see each other's faces when we looked into it. Then we wouldn't need to look at each other, we could just look into the mirror, wouldn't that be practical?«

»I don't think so, to tell the truth.«

»But smart, anyway?«

»It would more likely be crazy.«

»Thanks, Henrik, I didn't think you'd disappoint me.«

At first I thought more was coming, but he began to answer the letters I'd given him. I couldn't really concentrate on the bills I had to arrange in the ring binders, even though it was as easy as pie. I had a fair idea of what he was up to, but it was certainly strange to make comparisons to mirrors and that kind of thing.

At lunchtime a man in wranglers came in and installed the extension phone in the head clerk's office and attached it to the system that was there before. The boss has a phone connection to us because he's in an office divided from ours by the head clerk's office, and then we have a connection over to the other side of the hallway where the stock room is, otherwise we'd have to fling open the countertop and rush across the hallway every time we had something to say to the stock room manager.

When the wrangler had gone, the head clerk came out, rubbing his hands.

»That's that,« he said, satisfied, »now we don't need to sit and shout at each other anymore. Let's try it out.«

He's a little energetic dynamo of a man around forty. I don't like him because he has a talent for listening to you right up to the point where you begin to explain *why* something or other happened or didn't happen, then it's just as if he turned off a switch: All that doesn't interest me. How can you respect a man who, when it comes right down to the nitty-gritty, still won't listen to what you're saying about your good intentions? I easily begin to stutter when I go into his office with something, not because he's made fun of my earlier stuttering in any way, but because I stand there knowing that as soon as I begin to explain the matter, he will lean over his papers and become busy as hell.

Anyway, he went into the office and shut his door, which otherwise was always open to us, phoned out to us, and Toft answered with a sour expression.

A moment later he got up and opened the door into the head clerk's office without knocking. The head clerk tried to control himself.

»There's no harm in knocking, Toft.«

Toft played innocent.

»Excuse me, but, you see, the door is usually left open.«

»What do you want?«

»I have the figures you asked me to locate yesterday in connection with the sales drive in Hornsherred. The analysis we have is only nine months old, and it appears that about ten percent of the homebound housewives . . .

»Why don't you use the extension?«

»Oh, that's right, but we have to get accustomed to it, don't we?«

Toft went out again without shutting the door behind him. We sat in suspense for a moment, then the door was slammed from inside.

I understood Toft very well. He had always had that door standing open behind him so he could just go in to the head clerk every time anything came up, lean over his desk and chat away. Once his soul had arrived by later trolley, he didn't sit down much of the time. Either he stood over by me and chatted while he sorted something, or he went over to the stock room – – for you couldn't thrash everything out over the extension phone – – or he went in to see the head clerk and talked about customers who were difficult or customers who were good to deal with, or something that didn't have anything to do with the business at all, a play he'd seen in the theater, he loved to ransack a subject, unpack it like a Christmas present, one layer after the other, and the head clerk couldn't really stop him, partly because Toft wasn't just a trainee like me, but mainly because he could hook sentences together without periods or dashes so that all the while you had the feeling that now it was coming, that the next sentence was really important and strikingly true, and it was, often, but in such a way that it was clear that you hadn't heard the very best yet.

In a way I could understand the head clerk, even though he was a prick, for it was clear you couldn't sit there all the time and let yourself be entertained when there's work that's waiting. Maybe Toft liked to demonstrate, too, that the head clerk wasn't so much better than he himself when he could go right in like that and speak to him like a buddy, I think that's what it was that had become too much for him.

The stock room manager came up to the counter. A tall,

unkempt man; Toft said about him: He possesses a certain dull charm. I've included that in the book, too, not because it's something to aspire to but the turn of speech could be good to toss out sometime.

He laid some papers on the counter and then glared at the door to the head clerk's office.

»Well, really,« was all he said.

When he had gone, Toft said: Concise as a bottle opener.

I quickly wrote it down, at last there was something to go after.

When during the afternoon there was something to report to the head clerk, I was the one who had to say it over the extension phone. When once or twice the head clerk walked through, there was a chill in the room. I sat all the while anticipating a clash or at least Toft beginning to give a new lecture to me about mirrors and all that, but he did his work without a sound and didn't once come over and hang across my desk.

Then it was four o'clock. I went out to the toilet. Shortly after someone came into the stall next to me. I could hear from the clumsy movements and a particular kind of snort that is was Toft. I sat thinking about whether I should say anything, I really felt sorry for him. It didn't matter a bit to me, the telephone didn't affect me in the least, I was almost ecstatic over being freed from stuttering in the head clerk's office, yes, maybe I would be more able to tell him a couple of fine truths over the extension, even though he would probably interrupt before I got that far, yes maybe just sit giving his opinion into a dead phone while only Toft listened, maybe that would open his eyes to certain sides of me. But as we sat side by side with a thin dividing wall between us, I thought I had to say something or other, though without actually taking sides, to cheer him up anyway.

But then Toft said abruptly:

»Can you change hands without breaking the rhythm?«

I understood it was meant to be funny, but I thought it was very vulgar. Anyway, I never masturbated when someone sat on the adjacent toilet. I didn't say a word.

»Can't you see how rotten it is,« he continued, »there are five of us in the company and we have to sit and call each other over the telephone like soldiers at the front, can't you see what will happen to the atmosphere, the personal contact – –«

I shat on his personal contact.

»Maybe it's necessary in the large companies, but dammit that's why I got a job in a small company where you can talk together about things without buttons and wires. I don't care about this at all. I simply don't care. On the other hand, I'd also be ashamed to quit without a fight because there's really something very significant about the extension phone, can't you see that?«

He was getting excited, tore off paper furiously so it whirred and hummed on the roller.

»It's the cause of the individual to prevent that kind of thing from gaining a foothold. One should sabotage it. Tamper with the extension phone. Switch the wires so that he gets the stock room every time he calls the office. So he can really see he was barking up the wrong tree. So he has to contact us directly. It's up to us to put a stop to it. Where are you going from here?«

»I have to hurry home and eat and then go to class afterwards.«

»How about having a beer with me someplace so we can discuss what to do?«

I was just about to say yes when I remembered the dumb remark from just before and said that I didn't have time for it.

»Couldn't you skip for once or go a little later? I don't

want to tempt you to shirk your duty, but can't you see that this is much more important, this is decisive for the atmosphere in the company in the future − − if we let things slide we cooperate, so to speak, in the oppression of free speech, for what can we say over the extension phone? As soon as you come up with your opinion, he can just turn it off, can't you see that? Can't we just put our heads together for an hour, figure out something or other?«

I pulled the chain. When the roar came, I realized I shouldn't have done it. It was what I had longed for, that Toft would accept me, as a friend, as an adult, as a colleague, on equal footing, and then the whole thing was flushed away in this manner.

When the roar died away, I stood listening, but obviously he had gone. I went out and washed my hands, took out my blue book and began to write in it: Don't pay any attention to dumb remarks if − −«

Then I got mad and tore the damn book in two − − what good did it do me when what it contained always told me how I should not have been, never anything that could be used before it was all over and done with. I went into the toilet again, tossed it into the bowl and flushed. Of course it didn't go down. The hell with it. There was no name on it.

There was nothing amiss the next day. If only there had been. Toft was nice and friendly, answered the extension phone like a good boy, nearly too good.

He'll cut out one day. What the hell can I do? He doesn't care about me now, he's probably already applied for a new job, a company with only two people or something like that.

It was only at the lunch break that I discovered that I'd forgotten my bow tie. No one had said anything, they didn't care one way or the other about me, a bow tie more or less, that isn't noticed on the extension phone.

I ate hurriedly and went over to the department store. The receding hairline began scooping up.

»No, sir,« I said, »don't you have any neckties. But not too expensive.«

The Hot Water Bottle

I picked up the hot water bottle and unscrewed the black stopper. Then I turned on the cold water faucet and let the water run so that it could get even colder. It just managed to get ice-cold when I heard my wife's footsteps coming up the stairs. I hurried to fill the bottle and went in to the invalid.

Only her head showed above the quilt. Her old eyes followed me watchfully.

Here I am with your hot water bottle, I said gently. I placed it under her feet, observed for a moment the thin, crooked toes before I covered them again. She watched me attentively, but today there was no surprise in her look. I collected the magazines that lay on the quilt, walked around the room a bit, pushed a pair of shoes to the side and emptied an ashtray into the waste basket. As long as I walked around in there, she'd bite her teeth together so that I wouldn't hear her gasp. I opened a window, which was nearly torn out of my hands it was so windy.

»A little fresh air will soon make you well again,« I said, »and now a little music to cheer you up.«

She squinted very slightly when the noon concert poured in over her, but said nothing. As recently as a few days ago she had complained. She got a headache from the music and a sore throat when the window right behind her was open, but now she kept silent and watched me. I was onto her tactic. She didn't dare raise any new complaints because she knew I'd make use of them immediately, and at the same time stopped complaining about the things she had before so I'd believe they no longer bothered her and call off my encroachment.

»Call me if you need anything,« I said and went out, I closed the door and put my ear up against it. It was a while, but it came. First a long heaving gasp which was abruptly cut off, though, as if she knew I was listening. Another moment went by and then came the faint moaning in fits and starts, as if she didn't dare give it free rein, and after each interval the distinct chattering of teeth.

»What are you doing here?« my wife's voice sounded behind me, and I whirled around.

»I'm listening to the music,« I smiled. »It's much better from out here. Just listen.«

She listened a moment.

»Have you done it again?« she asked and looked at me with a little wrinkle between her eyebrows. »You're risking her health.«

»On the contrary,« I said. »She has been lying here for six months now without being really well, without being really sick, she could continue lying here like this for fifty years if we go on fussing over her.«

»It's the after-effects, her nerves,« whispered my wife.

»This isn't a mental clinic here, and I'm no psychiatrist. Half a year must be more than enough.«

»She needs nursing and loving care, this sort of thing takes time.«

»She needs to get really sick and be placed under professional care, and that's what I want to accomplish.«

»Let's go into the kitchen,« my wife said, »she can hear us here.«

We withdrew to the kitchen.

»Do you think I enjoy sleeping on the kitchen floor,« I said indignantly. »If we want to speak seriously with each other, we have to go into the bathroom, yes, not even seriously, just quite ordinarily, as we used to be able to sit and talk before. Now and then we'd shut up and look at a paper, then one of us would say something again, and the other would answer, and then a little time would pass again just sitting, it was cosy, what we said didn't need to be anything in particular, it was in a way signals we sent out just like ships meeting at sea, toot-toot, and then they sail on, but everything becomes nicer for a moment because you've just gotten a toot from the other ship. After she came it was destroyed.«

»She doesn't say anything.«

»She lies there listening. She pretends she's thinking about her own matters and stares up at the ceiling, but when you've spoken and I've spoken and we sit there again without saying anything, then she lies there getting excited, I can see her move her hands under the quilt, she blinks her eyes in a very intrusive way, it's quite clear that she's lying there thinking: Well, what of it?«

»It's your imagination.«

»There must be something more between these two people than just the single toots, she thinks, they must talk seriously and coherently once in a while, set aside what they have in their hands and get to the bottom of things. I wring and wrack my brain to find something important, that'll get you to look up and burst out: Oh you don't say! but it's hopeless, after a while I can't even say anything quite ordinary, I sit rigid and tense, waiting for you to say something that can loosen my tongue. All the warmth has vanished.«

»Dear, she's a sick old woman who's lost everything.«

»There must be institutions for her kind. Why should her sad fate infect our peaceful little world. I didn't ask her to come − −«

»You gave your permission, though.«

»That was just common decency. I thought it was a question of a few days until she'd found someplace to live – – she also talks about finding herself some easier work, but then she lies down instead.«

»She thought she could handle it. As long as she was on the move, on the run, she kept herself up, but as soon as she settled down here, she collapsed, it's completely understandable. But if you like, I can sleep in the kitchen.«

»And then I would have to sleep in her room – – and never get a wink's sleep. She'll have to move out here if there's not a change for the better or the worse soon.«

»We can't have her lying out here all day. Then we'd have to move her back and forth when I have to fix meals. But I don't understand why she hasn't said anything to me.«

»About what?«

»About your tactics.«

»That's easy. She's afraid you'll reproach me for something, then I'd get wind of her setting us up against each other and she'd have to leave the house. No, she's just as cunning as Gandhi, she tries her hand at passive resistance.«

»Here's your lunchbag. Now try to be in a little better mood before you get home, and knock that idea out of your head, won't you? – – What kind of funny suds are these in the cup?«

I stretched out my head while I put on my coat. – – »It looks like soap suds.«

»How in the world did soap suds get into the coffee cup?«

»Oh, now I understand why she said the coffee tasted of soap,« I said. »So I replied, that's not too good, she should get herself looked at if it kept up.«

My wife stared at me. I snatched my sandwich bag and hurried down the stairs.

In the evening I got cracking again. That morning I

hadn't asked if she wanted the hot water bottle changed. I'd simply taken it and returned with the remark: Here I am with your bottle. The matter was decided. But now I was sure she wouldn't say no so as not to complain – – so we still had to act out the little dumb play step by step, she a little step back, and I following. When my wife went out to wash up after the meal, I asked:

»Shouldn't I change the hot water bottle for you?«

She just nodded with rigid eyes. I ascertained a tiny sniffle, which didn't amount to anything, just a slight contraction of the nostrils which halted her breathing a second, and she smiled faintly as if she'd chalked up a point for herself. I paid no attention and pulled the hot water bottle from under the quilt. It was lukewarm, naturally my wife had changed it during the day. I went out to the bathroom and filled it with ice-cold water.

Later that evening I sat looking at the paper while my wife conversed in low tones with the old one. Clearly she'd gotten mail today, and my wife, who has a loveable and infallible way of satisfying her curiosity, hoped certainly that the letter contained something good? But no, it was from an acquaintance in Hamburg she'd written to. He'd heard, surely, of the flight, but had no information about the other refugees in the family. There was probably not much hope now.

Tomorrow I'll change my inquiry to: Do you mind if I refill your bottle? A small step each day.

Suddenly I had a suspicion. There was, perhaps, a little too lively ring to her voice in spite of the sorrowful words. I went over to the bed and hauled out the hot water bottle. The old one lifted her head from the pillow but let it fall back again right away. My wife looked pensively at the bottle. It was more than lukewarm. Without a word I went out to the kitchen with it.

A little later my wife came out.

»What's the meaning of this?« I asked, infuriated.

»Did you think I'd support you?« she asked calmly.

»No, but on top of that to cross my plans – –«

She began to rummage among the pans under the gas burners and got out a pan which she pumped half full of water.

»I don't recognize you,« she said. »I thought it was a whim. How can you do it?«

»Listen, it's us or her. We're still young and healthy, but she's stealing all our vim and vigor, so we'll end up being just as sick and helpless as she is. I'm doing it for our sake – – come here, sit up on the kitchen table beside me.«

We sat beside each other on the kitchen table. I took her hand. In the last six months it had been the usual prelude to our love-meetings which continued down on the kitchen floor beside the clothes basket that sometimes turned over and buried us with dirty socks and dishtowels.

»Don't you believe me?« I asked gingerly.

»I don't really know,« she answered dully. »I don't understand how one can love someone and at the same time kick another, who is weak and defenseless besides.«

»Yes, but that's exactly what one must do,« I explained. »To love a person is to prefer that person so much above all others that they can take a flying leap. And if they butt in anyway, they must be kicked aside.«

»That's not how I think of love,« she said. »To me to be in love is to be so full of tenderness and gratitude for what one is allowed to experience, that I have to pass it on to everyone I meet.«

»Then let me explain myself a little better,« I said. »Listen, a few days ago I intercepted a letter – –«

»No,« she gasped, »that can't be – – I can't believe that about you!«

I became a little confused.

»Intercepted sounds a little dramatic, maybe – – I just happened across a letter she'd gotten. Naturally I wouldn't have read it if I realized it was hers, you needn't worry. She'd forgotten it in one of her magazines.«

»But you must have seen right away that it wasn't to either of us, certainly her name was there at the top.«

»Well, yes, but I only discovered that later – – I simply sat browsing through this silly magazine, and then there was a piece of paper lying there, well, here's something' I just thought, and with no particular purpose I let my eyes run over the words since my eyes were already running indifferently over the pages until suddenly it occurred to me that, hey, the letter was certainly not meant for you, and it was only then I found her name at the top.«

»And then you put the letter down, I hope?«

»Naturally – – I mean . . .« I was irritated at the turn the matter had taken. Here I was about to justify myself, and then she managed to turn it against me. »At that point I'd already seen a great deal, to a large degree our future and happiness depended on it. You can't reproach a person for throwing his eyes open when he discovers something difficult and dangerous is heading toward him.«

»Naturally not,« she said impatiently, »tell me, what was it about?«

I felt relieved again.

»It was from a relative, I could see. In Hamburg. The writer expressed joy over the refuge she had found and the extremely friendly and comfortable treatment she'd received from us.«

»Well, there's nothing alarming in that.«

»But then it continues – – well, how did it go, oh, yes: We are looking forward to coming. Just like that.«

»For a visit probably.«

»For a visit – – from Hamburg – – do you think they're coming just to say hello and drink a cup of coffee and then take the night express back again?«

»You keep saying *they* – – I thought that she didn't have any connection with the rest of her family at all since the flight.«

»I don't know how many got away, but if there are only two or three of them, if there's only one it'll mean that it will be twice as impossible as it is now. We'll both have to sleep in the kitchen, and then should be grateful at that, maybe there's a grandmother and babies, all of them with shattered nerves and bedridden, all the drawers and shelves filled with screaming children. We'd have to be de-lighted if we could get the bathroom for ourselves, then we could take turns sitting and sleeping, and whenever an agreed upon time passed, e.g: an hour, the other would pull the chain.«

»Maybe something could be arranged in the attic storage room.«

»Are you crazy? Do you want to drive us mad?«

»I just don't understand why she didn't mention anything about it today when I talked with her.«

»It's very understandable, you know.«

I lifted up the hot water bottle and shook it in front of her so that it rippled. – – »Here you have the explanation. And if you just leave it to me, she'll get cold feet, I promise you, and warn them, yes, maybe she's already done it.«

She let herself slide down from the kitchen table, lit the gas and put the pan on. The table was cold and hard to sit on alone.

»I'd never have thought it of you. If I'd heard about it from others, I would have accused them of lying right to their bare faces, that you weren't like that. And now – –«

I noticed that she was crying and jumped down scared

from the kitchen table. I happened to push the hot water bottle so it plopped on the floor and lay there quivering for a moment, red and swollen, I picked it up, it was nearly cold again.

»Dear little darling,« I said. »I think you've misunderstood it completely . . .«

I stopped because I had no idea how to continue.

She was crying louder now that she'd realized I'd noticed it anyway.

»I just know that had I known it before we got married, then I wouldn't have gotten married.«

The water in the pan gave off a faint simmering sound.

Suddenly she shouted: »I won't be married to a hooligan!«

»But dear,« I said, startled, and put my arm around her shoulders. »You mustn't take it so literally – – did you really believe that I'd thought of chasing her away? I've only been teasing her a little because it seemed to me she'd begun to take all these things for granted, the hot water bottle every half hour, being served in bed, it almost reached the point that she began to grumble if we didn't immediately rush down Tuesday morning and get the new weekly magazine – – and so I wanted to teach her a lesson, one doesn't know what such stuff can lead to.«

She looked at me doubtfully.

»And the letter?« came the stifled words.

»Well,« I laughed, »I lied, it was just a whim. It irritated me that you sided with her, so I wanted to see how far you would go.«

»Does that mean that we don't have to expect a visit from her family?«

»Absolutely not. As far as I'm concerned, she can go on living here until the day she dies,« I asserted. »Besides I'm beginning to think that there's a certain charm with our

39

little detours out here, maybe we could even make it a little cosier, have a few paintings and such. I think we've had so many wonderful times out here already,« I said and tried to steal my arm in under hers, but she squeezed her elbow to her body.

»It isn't just that you lie to me and pull my leg,« she said, tired, »but you take it all back and make nothing of it as soon as you realize it's not going to get you anywhere, I call that despicable.« The water boiled, she tossed the brown coffee powder over the bubbles.

»What do you want me to do?« I shouted. »Would you rather I went on about her scrubby family?«

First the bubbles got viscous and calm, then the pan filled with airy light-brown foam. My wife stirred the foam with a wooden spoon.

»It's as if nothing really means anything to you, as if the truth is just a balloon you can alternately blow up and deflate.«

»You're making much too much of it. What's important is that we care about each other,« I said earnestly.

I picked up the hot water bottle, poured out the used water and filled it under the hot faucet.

»Look,« I said, »feel it, is it hot enough?«

She looked at me searchingly. I could see that she was already softening a little toward me. And I guess she had to feel a certain relief, too, that there was no danger of the apartment being converted into a refugee camp.

»I'll take it in now,« I said firmly.

I went in and lifted the quilt at the foot of the bed, put in the bottle, looked briefly at the yellowish, crooked toes with ingrown nails before I let the quilt drop.

»Can't we turn the music down a little,« said the old woman with her suffering voice.

I looked amazed at her.

40

»But the radio isn't even on,« I said.

»I can hear music, it's giving me a headache.«

»It must be the neighbor's radio,« I said, »we can't do anything about that.«

I sat down to look at one of her women's magazines, but couldn't really concentrate on it. Now the radio next door seemed a bit too annoying, to me, too. Maybe we could go over and ask them to turn it down a little. Or put some cotton in both our ears.

My wife came in with the full tray.

»Now let's have a proper cup of coffee,« she said. She was still red around the eyes, but smiled at us. She wanted to do her best to make things good between the three of us. Relieved, I put down the magazine and helped her serve from the tray.

»I think it's cold in here,« said the old woman, »maybe there's an open window someplace?«

»Not in here,« I said. I went in to the kitchen, but the window there was completely shut, too. I came back and sat down without saying anything. The old woman lay crying silently.

»What's the matter?« my wife asked kindly.

»It's the coffee,« the patient sniffled.

»Isn't it good?« my wife asked, astonished, »it's just been freshly made. I myself think it's quite good.« She looked at me: – – »What do you think?«

»I haven't tasted it yet,« I said, and put sugar in it.

»It tastes of soap,« whimpered the old woman.

I had lifted my cup halfway to my mouth, but set it down again. My wife stared at her half-filled cup with surprise and disgust.

The old woman turned her head toward the wall.

»Me feet are so cold,« she said.

Strangle the Bantams

Snow in the middle of April, isn't it impertinent. And the worst of it is you can't take your eyes off it. Is there anything sadder than a thin dose of snow which won't amount to anything anyway. You sit and stare, and the coffee sits there getting cold. You'll probably have to make a little more coffee, Annie, no, not right now – – first you must tell me something to get my mind off the idiotic snow. And the stupid bantam chickens. Aren't you going to wring their necks soon? I'm tired of forever and ever seeing them walk scratching the earth in their miserable pen. Or let them go, so they can get run over, so at least they've had that experience.

If you're going to make more coffee anyway, then make it black this time. I said *black*. As thick as tar, not the usual dishwater you produce – – yes, I know you mean well by me; my heart, my fat, and all that – – but just do me a favor and mean bad by me for once and brew a really poisonous coalblack coffee.

You always think I'm hiding something from you. Haven't you always gotten the report sooner or later? It's actually becoming a habit. First one little secret a week, then two, and now we've come to the point that if I arrive some Sunday without having some juicey sins to confess, you immediately get the entire lot of withdrawal symptoms: nausea, paleness, dizziness, sweating fits, hallucinations and attacks of anxiety, until finally I have to make something up so you can recover again.

Have I hurt you again. Annie, you little fool, I've never pulled your leg. I'm just talking about what might happen if you don't restrain yourself a little. But really you must be able to see that. I'm glad to have you to confide in, I just can't stand having it dragged out of me. There, drink your coffee now, at least you can tolerate it. But still, remember to eat a little in between, won't you — — not just when I come? I don't want to sit here eating the whole cake, take a piece yourself. I don't mean you're too thin, I think you look wonderful just as you are, but we'd hate to have you end up nothing but skin and bones.

I have what you're fishing for. Why do you think I brought him up — — just to make you curious and nothing else? I can assure you: I haven't lost my heart, I haven't prom- ised to marry him, he hasn't duped me out of my savings, and I have little respect left for him or his type, even though I still . . . well, we'll get to that.

Ugh, those clotheslines that hang there clacking their naked clothespins against each other. If you haven't got anything washed, couldn't you at least hang up some dirty clothes so something would hang there waving. And this bantam rooster, it's the dumbest thing I've ever seen. Every twenty minutes it trudges up on one of the hens like on a scale, three seconds later it gets off and walks away self-sat- isfied, while the hen shakes herself a little and continues scratching. New egg on the way. Well, it will soon get dark now, I hope.

You're peeved that I go to Gerda's parties and don't try to get you to go with me, but as sure as I'm sitting here in my own fat person, you wouldn't get a thing out of it. In the first place you'd be scandalized at a lot of things, and if not, these people would see to it that you were. They have their own ways and you have to take it or leave. In the second place you'd immediately get ploughed to the gills. I know that no one can drink you under the table with coffee, but it's quite a long while between coffees in that world. And the next day you'd be disgusted with yourself, and particularly at everything you had missed while you'd slept it off. Just think if someone had made a pass at you while you didn't know where you were, that would be a shame. Well, have I hit too close to home again — — just don't give it a damn. But in short, I think you'll get more out of what I tell you about it. Come on, give Trille a little smile, and she will give you some details. I always try to get it all in, it's my goal to be able to relate something so elaborately some day that you simply won't have anything to ask about afterwards. You'll just have to stop staring at those bantams every time I mention Gerda. And Preben.

He's all right in his way. Not terribly bright, the opinions he tosses out he's stolen from letters to the editor the same day. Not handsome but quite attractive. Slightly balding and stooping, but he has something that can distract the ladies — — I wonder what it really is, I think his eyes, they're nice, good-natured, a little ingenuous. God knows whether seducers are themselves aware of what it is the girls fall for — — they go to dances, bodybuilding and become educated as attractive fellows, turn on the ardent glance when they come across a good one, but when they inadvertently happen to relax once in a while, you can almost get weak in the knees when you discover that there can be some wonderful fellows behind their neckties. Well, of course it might be part of their strategy, you can never be too sure. But anyway, Preben. By now I've got him psyched out at these parties, and what irritates me is he always has to demonstrate to the whole world that girls fall for him. Well, he tries to be discreet, but it's only a clumsy imitation of the really discreet seducer, which you never see in action, and whom everyone knows is dangerous for women. For certain women, Annie. Stop stirring your coffee, look at your bantams instead. But when Preben has brought someone or other down, or wherever it is he drops them – – we found one on a hanger in the cloak room, but by the way it wasn't one of his – – then he always tries to return at just the right moment. I think he simply stands waiting outside the door until it's relatively quiet, preferably when the rest of them are engaged in a very intense discussion and turn off the phonograph – – then he comes in as if by accident, remains standing there, seemingly distracted, in the doorway – – til he is sure that everyone has seen him – – then hurries over to the group in discussion and little by little joins in the discussion, but to be on the safe side he makes sure to choose the right strategic moment to become a little distracted, look dreamy and forget to answer, then smiles shyly and asks: »Pardon me, what was that you said?« And then there's always some bungler who claps him on the shoulder and says: What's the matter with you, old boy, what have you been up to now? – – And *only then* will he suddenly become attentive and braid his letter-to-the-editor opinions into the strangest contexts. Good grief, is it any wonder that I kept my eyes open? I am ratified as the fat funny girl of the party. They flock to me when they have nothing else to do. For some reason or other everything sounds much funnier when it bubbles up through a mountain of flesh like me, I can get them to gape at me and listen to me and get drinks for me, but none of them would dream of kissing me or blocking my view in other ways, so I see more than most.

Now don't say that I have nice legs anyway. You have damn nice arms, you should just watch out they don't get thinner than they are. Mind your meals. Eat some of your bantam-chuck-chuck-eggs instead of giving them to your neighbors. How about a bantam omelette?

Besides, I saw others than just him, too, but you've heard all that before. The unknown young poet who got up and

recited his hitherto most unappreciated poem without no-
ticing that his muse disappeared into the greenhouse with a
student actor – – but I guess she'd probably heard the poem
before. A young tightfitting woman discussed South Africa
with a Chinese man while her husband managed to climb
up two lamp stands, munch several hyacinth bulbs, take
Gerda out in the coatroom for fifteen minutes – – yes, by
the way, it was she who hung on the coat hanger when we
went to get our coats in the morning – – whereupon he
came back and broke right into the middle of a discussion
about the Common Market with the words: Einstein was all
right! and fell into a trance behind the piano with an iron
sculpture on top of him. It was fun, the people were honestly as mad as hatters, and I think they got something good
out of it in some way, but the way Preben acted was enough
to make you puke. I told him so when he sat down at the
piano and played. He lives it up on these same four melo-
dies: Hide Your Kisses, I Wonder Who's Kissing Her Now,
Smoke Gets In Your Eyes, and Ave Maria. Oh, I know it's
your repertoire, too, Annie, but that's not what concerns us
right now. I let myself bulge in over the upright piano, and
he looked up with his good-natured, self-effacing smile.

»What about expanding your repertoire?« I asked.

»What do you want to hear?« he asked and fondled the
keys.

»Do you know this one: Just a gigolo . . .«

»I'm not sure if I remember that one,« he said and tried
to look as if he were concentrating.

»That doesn't matter in the least,« I broke in. »Do you
know what you are? In the first place you're stupid. But
that's all right, too.«

He got so flustered that he began to play a homemade
hymn with crossed hands.

»The sad thing is that you're ridiculous, too. What is it you want us to think of you? That you're irresistible? That you do it pretty good? Or that you're fairly well-endowed?«

Then I turned my broad back on him and surrendered myself to the morning coffee. That's the best thing about such a party. You drink and put on an act for twelve hours, say and hear a lot of nonsense, and then suddenly it's light, you haven't slept and aren't sleepy, your tongue is just like emery cloth, and then the coffee comes, a real eye-popping coffee, it's enough to give you religion. Glasses and guests lie all around, only three or four people are still sitting with rigid eyes and beer all over their clothes, someone salvages croissants and hardrolls around the corner, you sniff in forward and dig in on the rolls, you've survived, you are round and sound. Your arms and legs are about where they should be, your clothes are only a little wrinkled, you drink your coffee, your heart kicks up its heels like an old circus horse, and then out into the air, that's the most wonderful, the mist, drenched branches in the yards, birds that stare at you with big surprised eyes, the sound of your own trudging down the flagstones, a trolley yawns noisily and un-embarassedly in a curve, I always walk on a morning like that – – alone, Annie – – the drops on the telephone wires, the moisture that settles in your hair, on your glasses, on your tongue – – and maybe you get a glimpse of a blood-shot sun through a naked hedge, too – – I feel new-washed through and through and go right home to bed, wake four hours later all alone without a hangover, think about going out to you in the afternoon and telling you all about it, pluck the newspaper out of the mail slot, treat myself to coffee in bed, lie there pampering myself until I have to leave, I always look forward to coming here, I think it's cosy here. I know I normally criticize, the curtains are too sickly-pink, the wallpaper pattern too glossy or I suddenly get mad at your paintings, − − but it doesn't matter, the atmosphere's cheerful and nice, that's the most important thing for me. That you are the one who lives here. I wouldn't miss any of it, except for your fine feathered friends out there. We're the only ones from the old gang who still hang out together, Annie.

Then one day the doorbell rang, and there he stood outside with a bouquet of tulips. It always makes me laugh when people bring me flowers, you know flowers and I just don't agree, a half hour after they come in the house they have a complete collapse − − either I've forgotten to put the water in the vase or I put them in a bottle which turns out to hold turpentine or stain remover − − I buy loads of potted plants every week − − not because I like them, I can't stand them, that's what's wrong, I suppose − − but I honestly try to make the place look like a kind of home − − some need a lot of water, others just a little, some need to be in the shade, others need to have ultra-violet light or hormones, I can never remember which need what and how often, you should see what a cartload of withered rubber trees and hanging plants I toss out every week − − at it again, out and buy new ones − − I'm the florist's solace in bad times. − − But anyway, there stands this fellow Preben, and bows well-groomed, I get the flowers set in for their demise, offer him a beer, but he doesn't want any.

»Spit it out,« I say, »if I've offended you, you'll get an apology − − but I won't guarantee what I'll say the next time I get a little high.«

No, I haven't offended him in the least, he asserts. On the contrary, he has thought a great deal about what I said and tried to figure out what was wrong with him.

He sits there about to drown in my big wing back chair, you know, the one I used to call the carnivore. It's there I like to seat people I fear will suddenly begin leaping up and giving a lecture – – it's not possible to get up by yourself, I nearly have to throw a line down to them when they have to leave. He came out with a touching story about his former wife who was so lovely and sensible and really good at making split-pea soup, but one day there came a big bad wolf and ate her up. When he got to that point, he wanted the beer after all.

And now he had gone and found out that it was for that reason he behaved the way he did. The big bad wolf had had something that his wife couldn't resist, and he strained to live up to that in relation to others, he wanted to impress people as a ladykiller, gain a reputation for it, so his wife could get wind of it and think: By God, if I'd only known that.

I said to him: Can't you see, it's really crazy, boy? Do you want to revenge yourself on your wife by taking it out on half-drunk, blameless girls? I'm sorry to say, but if it's my blessing you want, this is where I get off.

No, no, he could see that was entirely wrong, too; I had struck him right in the solar plexus, but he couldn't see how to tackle the matter now.

»Tell me, does your wife still go with the other fellow?«

No, it hadn't really worked out.

»Then why not try going back to her,« I said. But he didn't want to go back to her. It was degrading, he explained. The thing he suffered most from wasn't exactly a sense of proportion.

»But then you must try to find a new wife and get this delayed adolescence over with.«

No, there could be no talk of that, either. There was no one who could replace her.

»Then I don't know. Try something completely different, then. You can blow smoke rings, for example, train yourself to be a genius at smoke rings, there aren't many who get very far in that field − − it's enough to tackle for a smart guy.

If he hadn't sat in the carnivore he would have leaped on his knees before me, but now it only amounted to a little wriggling, it took something from the effect, you know. Yes, I would have to help him. Save him, I believe by God he said. I'd gotten him to see things clearly, but he had no idea what he should do with his clear sight, therefore I should take care of him and get him to see still more clearly. He despised himself, but I should wash and press his rumpled ego, sew buttons and zippers on his psyche.

»Not with me,« I said decidedly. »Nil. I have my friends to look after; just because in mixed company I happen to speak a few civil words to you, I certainly won't take the rap for it afterwards.«

Then he got quiet in the chair.

»Here, have another beer,« I said, »and then you should go home and think everything over. When all is said and done, you yourself are the only one from whom you can get assistance.

A little later he said just as quietly: »I don't feel very well.«

I got a little nervous, I'd hate to have him make some sort of blunder, but I didn't say anything.

Then there came again from the very bottom of the chair: »I don't feel very well.«

What should I have said, Annie? In any case, I said then:

»You can drop by another time, if you like. Without flowers.«

So that's the lay of the land then. Since then he has popped up every few days, sits talking a while, quite sensibly, without our really getting anywhere. Sometimes he perks up a bit and sends me one of his searching glances, it isn't easy to break the habit, I guess, but he checks himself.

Naturally you think I've been to bed with him, but I really haven't. But then again, I may do it one day. In the long run, it won't be enough for you to sit staring at the three-second rooster, either. I would go stark raving mad from it, I think I'd begin to say squawk-squawk and lay cracked eggs everywhere.

Perhaps that would get him over the dead point. I think he'd get his self-respect back by doing a good deed for a middle-aged fat girl like me.

Well, Annie, eat your cake. I'll take you along to one of the parties if you really want to go. But wouldn't it be better if we took a trip south together like we did five years ago? This time we'll just arrange it a little better. Strangle those bantams and let's go. I'll be sure to dig something up for you. Loose or steady. Drink your coffee now, take the last piece of cake. You must try to flesh out a bit before we travel. That business with him is not a matter of life and death to me, and afterwards we'll go down south, won't we? Yes, thank you, one more cup. This is what I call real coffee.

Layer Cake

And here's the living room. You'll see in a little while, if you
stay that long, it's sunny in here from three o'clock and on
through the rest of the afternoon − − when there is sun,
that is. No, there's no bathtub, but that's the sort of thing I
don't think you'll miss when you haven't got it in the first
place. The vegetable store is across the street, and over
there is the delicatessen − − his liverpaste isn't always up to
par, but all he needs is to be told off once in a while. The
bakery is at the next corner; I was a regular customer there
for many years, but not any more, though you don't need to
feel any obligation on that score. Their bread was excellent.
On Sundays we liked to have cookies with our afternoon
coffee and Dam, the baker, made them just right − − you
know slightly sticky inside. First we'd stand outside the
bakery looking at what was in the window, and I'd ask:
»How about some coffee-cake, Henry, wouldn't that be nice
for once? Or almond sticks?« Sometimes, when we were
feeling really crazy we might even say, »How about a big
nasty napoleon?« − − I hope I don't offend you, it wasn't
meant that way of course. »Or a chocolate eclair?« But we
were used to being thrifty from our early years together, so
we ended up with cookies. Nevertheless, I've asked him − −
not once, but hundreds of times − − if he wouldn't like to
have a piece of layer cake. I certainly wouldn't have be-
grudged him that, he was so thin and hollow-cheeked that I
was almost ashamed to be seen with him on the street. I always made sure that he wore at least two sweaters under
his coat to make him look a bit more impressive, so a few
calories would have become him. But, »No-o-o,« he always

said, »it's too rich for me.« So, it's no wonder that I believed him and kept on buying cookies, is it?

The years went by and he got thinner and thinner; I put up with it, padded him well with woolen sweaters and scarves when we went out. His head, I couldn't do much about, of course, but with his collar well pulled up under his chin and his hat down over his eyes, nobody noticed anything.

Things went neither better nor worse than that my sister on Amager had a big party one Saturday, and I did all the cooking, and they were so pleased and ate so well that when they got to the coffee and layer cakes hardly anyone could eat another bite, and I ended up getting some pieces of the cake to take home with me.

The next day was Sunday, and at three o'clock Henry started to put on his sweaters and coat as usual, and I say: »Where are you going?«

»Aren't we going over to the bakery?« he asks.

»Not today,« I tell him, »we've still got some layer cake left over from yesterday, so just take off your coat again.«

But when I set the cake down in front of him, he gets even more quiet than usual and just stares at it.

»What's wrong?« I ask.

»Nothing, except that I can't eat it.«

Here I must add that it was a beautiful cake with very fine texture, several layers of different jam fillings and a thick layer of whipped cream on top and it was decorated with orange slices and bits of chocolate and colored candies.

»What kind of nonsense is that?« I said. »Here we haven't had layer cake for twenty-one years, and when I finally give you a piece, you can't eat it.«

»I never liked layer cake,« he says looking down.

»Well I never,« I say to him. »Here am I offering you

something really delicious, instead of those same old cookies, and then you tell me that you don't like it. Maybe you want me to eat it − − me, with my figure; you're the one who really needs it.«

But he looked so guilty that I didn't suspect anything, so I just said, »well, we'll try a little later then.«

When it was time for coffee that evening I set out the layer cake again, and this time I took a piece for myself to sort of encourage him a little. Well, he did take a bite too, but sat for a long time turning it around and around in his mouth. »Come on, man, swallow,« I said. He did, and then he put down his fork.

»What's wrong with you?« I asked. »Am I supposed to sit here alone eating this cake, which isn't even good for me.«

»It's too rich for me,« he said, »you know that.«

Well now, I'd like to ask you when a man who hasn't had a decent piece of layer cake in twenty-one years finally gets a piece, why can't he eat it? I think there can be only one answer: Somehow he's had enough layer cake. Anyone else would dig right in, even if he knew it would just go to his waistline, but he − − who was skinny as a skeleton − − he pushed it away.

So the question was: Where would somebody be fed so much layer cake that he couldn't get a bite of it down at home? Who can afford to stuff so much that he actually becomes nauseated by it − remember, layer cake isn't cheap these days. I can only see one explanation: a woman who works in the bakery. With a job like that, a woman can always figure out a way when she gets a crush on a man. And here for twenty-one years, Sunday after Sunday, he had insisted that he didn't want any layer cake, that it was too rich for him − − and I'd fallen for it every time, gullible as I am.

But nevertheless, I wanted to give him a chance, since

we'd stuck together for so long, after all there are things that create bonds – – memories and so forth. So when he came home from work the next day I asked as usual: »Are you hungry?«

»You bet, what have you got to offer?«

»Fried flounder, good and fresh. But first you have to eat your cake from yesterday, otherwise it'll get stale.«

He got a very strange look on his face.

»Yes, but if I don't like layer cake . . .« He said. But now I let him have a piece of my mind.

»Look here,« I said, »I don't know where you go and eat your layer cake, and I couldn't care less how much cake you eat when you're not at home. But if that makes you think you can turn up your nose at my layer cake, you've got another think coming.«

He didn't know what to do with himself, and asked me to explain what I meant.

»I don't think I need to go into details,« I just said.

So he himself took the plate with his piece of cake, and carried it into the living room. When I went in after a little while, the plate was already empty. But I wasn't completely convinced, because when one has eaten layer cake, there are usually a few smears here and there on the plate, yet this plate was practically clean. I should really have gone back to the flounder again, but I stayed in the living room dusting a bit and so forth. I looked in the wastebasket, I checked the cupboards, and then I thought of looking inside the wood-burning stove, and sure enough, there it lay, a pretty sight, with the whipped cream downwards.

I went into the kitchen and got another piece of cake.

»Now you eat it, while I'm watching you,« I said.

»And if I can't?«

»You can't, eh? But when you are with your bakery

woman it's no problem − − there you can stuff yourself so much that it's impossible to get another piece down, even if it's you very own wife who is offering it to you.«

»Ba-bakery woman?« he stammered.

»Yes,« I said, »bakery woman.«

He wanted to say something, but his mouth just opened and closed a couple of times, then he picked up the fork again.

»There's no need to look like that,« I said. »I haven't put poison in it − − not yet.«

Suddenly he began stuffing it into himself in huge heaps and as soon as he had finished he rushed out of the room and threw up.

Well, if that isn't proof, I don't know what would be. Just imagine. He had such an overdose of layer cake at that bitch's place that eating one more piece made him throw up. And as if that wasn't enough, he didn't want any flounder either. They must have been some orgies they had! And here I've been waiting on him and darning his socks and looking after his goldfish for twenty-one years and I just thought he was a little slow. And then, in the course of twenty-one hours, an abyss of deceit suddenly opens up.

From then on, not a day went by that I didn't buy layer cake and force it into him.

I clearly remember the last day he was at home when he said,

»As long as I've got to eat something I don't like, can't you buy napoleons instead? I don't care for them either, but I think I could keep them down better.«

At that point I lost my patience:

»That's what you'd like, eh? First gorge yourself on layer cake outside, and then continue with napoleons here at home − − no sir, I'll have no respect for you until the day you ask me yourself for your layer cake here, in your own home.«

He sat for a long time staring straight ahead, took a bite now and then, and when he had eaten half of the piece, he left the room. I thought he was just going out to throw up as usual, but he didn't come back. The next day his sister sent me a message saying he had moved in with her. Of course, he still has to pay me something but even so, it still doesn't add up to enough so I can afford to stay in a big apartment alone. That's why I want to exchange apartments with you.

I've seen him a couple of times since; it was something of a shock, he'd almost gotten fat. I don't think that was very nice of him. It's as though he was showing that he hadn't gotten any decent food during those twenty-one years, and I have his own word that he did: »You're a good cook, at least one has to admit that,« he used to say. The food just didn't stick to his ribs. Not before he moved.

It won't be easy to give up this window here. Perhaps I should tell you what he looks like, and maybe you could write to me if he passes by once in a while. That way it wouldn't seem as though I'm completely out of the picture.

Besides, I'm not really sure I want to exchange apartments with you. Your apartment isn't very big; I don't know how I'll find room for the furniture. But, anyway, I've got your telephone number, so I'll let you know one of these days. But, as I said I don't think − − yes, of course, I won't keep you then; I need to pick up a few things myself before the stores close − − I'll see you out.

The Matches

Recently I've tramped around a good deal, but it doesn't do much good any more; these days you can't go anywhere without meeting someone. It's the increase in the population. I don't know how many billions we are on earth at the moment, and in twenty-five years God knows how many we'll be, that's what my wife says, anyway. And the more there are the fewer each. It's just like the krone which is worth less and less, it will get to be small change, all of it. Soon no one will take the trouble to bend down for a five øre piece lying on the sidewalk. The time it takes to bend down and straighten up again – – it just doesn't pay nowadays. Not to mention two øre pieces. I feel rather like a two øre piece now. One without a hole.

Soon you won't be able to take a step without meeting someone. At home I never see a soul. Yes, I am, in a way, married. My wife and I knew each other very well. She was a younger woman, until recently, anyway. I haven't been home for fourteen days. Just tramped around practicing the list of kings. Once in a while there's a tingling in the soles of my feet, and then you think about how things will go when you get older and can't walk so well. Usually I'm got nervous about growing old, the only thing that can give me sleepless nights once in a while is the thought of becoming 66. 65, that's quite all right, it's something you have to go through, and 67, or for that matter 76 or 77, it's just natural, but 66 gives me goose bumps, I think there is something derogatory in becoming 66. It will just be nice when it's over and done with and you can look people in the eye again.

Now you mustn't think that there's anything at all between me and my wife. I've profited greatly from knowing her. I've gotten a great deal of information from her. For example, it was she who taught me the difference between a man and a woman. It's not at all as simple as it sounds. I'm afraid, too, that I've forgotten it in the meantime. It was a while before I figured it out, but she was very persevering. Just don't give up, she said.

It was something about matches. A man strikes a match in one way, either down or up the striking surface, but a woman does it in reverse, the reverse of one of the two methods, then. I can't really remember which now. Maybe I could figure it out if I had some matches on me, but I don't smoke. In fact, it's a fairly important problem, that difference, and what will happen when everyone has switched to lighters? There's something that will be lost there.

Really I should get myself a box of matches, but what would I use all the others for? You could, of course, give the box away afterwards – – to someone over eighteen – – but wouldn't it seem a little strange to give away a box of matches when one of them was used? Maybe it might be thought that you weren't really satisfied with the quality. Or should I begin to smoke, then, but that's a big step to take at my age. By that, of course, I mean the age I am right at the moment – – you never know how things will stand later on, but maybe later on can last a long time.

You could also ask for a match, but then you'd have to hasten to add that you didn't want it lit, for then it wouldn't matter. I'm just afraid that people would be astonished if you asked them for a match and then walked away with it. Maybe they would begin to follow you – – and when there are already so many people on the street . . .

Besides, you'd have to have a matchbox, too. Naturally it need only be a used one, but it seems to me it's been a long

59

time since I've seen empty matchboxes lying in the street – – or any matchboxes at all, for I've never looked to see if they were empty – – but it certainly would be most unusual if there were any, wouldn't it?

I'd like to know what people do with their used matchboxes if they don't throw them away. Maybe keep small things in them, buttons, Christmas seals, baby teeth. I think it's a strange mania, but that's their own business, it's just that it inhibits me in my development.

Well, no one says that you have to develop yourself all through your whole life, either; anyway, I got sufficiently developed during the time I was with my wife. I would just like to get the problem cleared up once and for all, and then I had thought of stopping my development.

So maybe it would be best to drop by home for a minute because I know my wife has matches there – – if the apartment hasn't been modernized in the meantime so that they've switched to central heating. But it would be strange if such a box of kitchen matches ran out the same day they put central heating in.

Only, the problem is: What will I say when I go home? When you're at home, you don't need to say anything, my wife was satisfied if I just nodded once in a while, all in all it was a very idyllic relationship. I just got confused a little about the thing with the matches, and then I wanted to go for a walk to gather my thoughts, and you know how time flies, suddenly fourteen days have gone by, and then it's as if you have to have something new to tell when you step in the door, and it's so difficult to have something new to tell a wife who's so up on everything. Even about the population increase; I've considered it, but *that* she's been aware of for a long time. That's what I've always said, she says.

I don't know if there's any use telling her about the fire I witnessed in Vanløse a few days ago. There were both fire engines and firemen or the like, but it was only a casserole that was on fire.

Well, maybe I should venture homewards. Maybe I could make my wife suspect that I was the one who set the fire. It's possible, too, that I might find a box of matches on the way home, one can always hope.

Cachet

It distresses me that I look like other people. I'm not going so far as to say that I look like all other people, there are a number of people who look quite different, I don't resemble them, but then there is the great multitude who more or less look like each other. It's them I look like. More or less. That distresses me.

One can describe my appearance in two ways: my friends say that I look rather ordinary, my enemies say I am a common type. There the descriptions end. Like everyone with no particular characteristics I am in fact indescribable.

I'm not ashamed of looking like other people. That would be undemocratic. It's just that it distresses me. The other day I was at a party where there were a number of people I didn't know and who didn't know me, either. Nevertheless one guest said, when we were introduced to each other: »It seems to me that I've seen your face somewhere.« »It's very possible,« I said courteously, »a few years ago I was a waiter on the Great Belt ferry.«

But it turned out that the man had resided on Ær Island for many years and hadn't been off the island until he'd moved into this town a few days before. I had to regret that I had never set foot on Ær Island.

»Haven't you family on Ær Island, a brother or a sister?«

»I have a brother, to be sure, but he lives on Bornholm and doesn't look like me at all.«

»Then you must have a double, I've seen you before anyway.«

The distressing thing is that you can be confused with

others, and others can be confused with you. It often happens that complete strangers greet me on the street, shouting: »Hi, Søren,« or »We enjoyed the other evening, Danielsen, say hello to your aunt for me!« and I haven't the slightest idea whether I should return these greetings or not. On the other hand, my acquaintances often come out with sour remarks like: »Well, obviously you don't care to say hello when someone meets you on the street.«

»I hope you'll excuse me,« I answer, blushing. »I didn't know I'd met you on the street recently, where could that have been?«

»Yesterday afternoon on the Walking Street,« comes the answer, or: »Sunday outside the Zoo.«

When I then assert that at the time in question I was busily occupied with painting the kitchen or digging in the garden, it's invariably taken as a poor excuse.

It's not a question of one, but of hundreds, thousands of doubles. Thousands upon thousands of people are quite ordinary in appearance and they get along excellently, as far as I can see. Maybe some of them go to the movies and dream starry dreams on the way home, but then when they get home and drink tea with their spouses, they think: No, it's too high a price with all the publicity-nuisance, pestered by journalists, fan letters, a private phone number, divorces, gossip columns, bad nerves, it's really much better and healthier to be able to relax without being stared at. I'm of the same opinion myself, still I can't help asking my wife now and then if she wouldn't have preferred a husband with slightly more marked features or an otherwise distinct appearance. She immediately answers with an emphasis that leaves no doubt about her sincerity: Absolutely not! I like you just as you look, you have just the appearance I can't resist.

For the moment it has a very calming effect, but the next second a cold chill runs down my back, for the answer could mean that she looked with the same affection on my thousands of doubles and it was only due to pure chance that she hit on me – – possibly it wouldn't have happened if we hadn't met one another. And given bad luck she could have gone and fallen in love with one of my many potential rivals. I became anxious about our happiness and began to keep my eye on her when we were out. Every time I saw her talking to a common type, I tried to get her away from him with some excuse or other and introduce her to interesting personalities with more distinctive appearances instead. The first time she became rather surprised at my sudden solicitude, but apparently not dissatisfied.

I realized that now it was high time to make a serious effort. I tried to look at it practically. It wasn't a matter of changing appearance, which in the first place was impossible, unless I ate myself fat or starved myself or disfigured my face by taking part in traffic accidents, and in the second place it wasn't desirable since my wife after all did prefer just my present appearance. It should only be a matter of a slight change, a single little cachet, not too conspicuous, so that she would still be fond of me, yet evident enough that she'd be able to recognize me among many others. What wouldn't I have given for a tiny innocent pimple on my forehead, a crooked tooth, a single bat ear!

Now, I'm quite interested in sports without being myself an active sports fan, and it couldn't escape my attention how training gives boxers and wrestlers more powerful torsos and arm muscles, cyclists more powerful leg muscles etc., with training you could do something with your body, why shouldn't you also be able to train your face, which is only a small part of the whole, after all, even though the part by which you first judge a person. I began my face-training, sat for hours before the mirror and studied distinctive facial expressions and soon succeeded in finding one I thought suited me well without distorting my original appearance: I wrinkled my brow so one of my eyebrows was a little higher than the other, simultaneously twisting the corners of my mouth in a way that invested me with a pained expression as if I had been exposed to cruel trials of fate. With persistent training I succeeded in maintaining this interesting expression longer and longer, finally for nearly three days, but then my wife suggested that I take a few days off from work because I looked so exhausted. And since these dislocations in my natural, ordinary facial expression gave me constant headaches, it was with a certain relief that I gave up this course of action in favor of the inner method.

The face is the mirror of the soul. Now and then you see faces which in their very features and proportions do not differ from the majority yet still distinguish themselves by something unusual, something in their glance, a form of radiance which must come from within, behind the exterior face, from a spiritual power center, which must be shaped and strengthened by strong inner experiences, protracted thinking, serious scruples great resignation. I immediately took up that way, purchased books on strange religions and ancient mystics, ground away at the great philosophers from Plato to Kierkegaard in the late night hours. In the beginning I was still too impatient. Every time a great thought had dawned on me and pulled the bottom out from under my way of life up to then, I rushed to the mirror to see if my spiritual tremor hadn't set its mark upon me. Every time I turned back equally disappointed to the desk and began my next spiritual crisis. But before this method managed to bear fruit, something happened which made me forget Eastern philosophers and the mystics of the Middle Ages.

65

At a party I had as usual rescued my wife from a man who reminded me of myself to an unbearable degree and steered her over to a famous editor whose sarcastic remarks, Mephistophelean eyebrows and long nose seemed to me to inspire more confidence. Shortly after that I was with another woman, deeply engrossed in Eastern mysticism, when our host came over to me and whispered:

»You're really brave, aren't you?«

»What do you mean?« I asked.

»I saw you personally lead her right into the lion's mouth. I wouldn't dare leave my old grandmother alone with that scribbler for two minutes.«

»Alone, there are a lot of people here,« I said calmly.

»They've been out in the garden about a quarter of an hour − − or wherever they've been. What he can accomplish in a quarter of an hour is no mean feat, that I can promise you.«

»Oh,« I said casually, »my wife's got grit. Besides, he isn't her type at all.«

»I just mention it because it annoys me − − you know I'm a little gone on your wife myself.«

Smiling, I reassured him and disposed of him and tried to collect my thoughts on Buddha and Tao again, but soon realized that life on earth still had too strong a grip on me and excused myself from my female disciple by saying I had to go out and pee. However, I went over to the glass door leading out to the garden and was about to open it when I heard a woman's voice behind me say:

»Oh, there you two are, where have you been?«

I turned and saw my wife and the editor come in and sit down at a crowded table. I observed my wife's face searchingly. Weren't her cheeks a little redder than normal, wasn't there more lustre in her eyes, didn't her lips swell a little more than usual? Yes, indeed, but I had to admit that she usually looked like that after several hours of a lively party with wine and dancing, so I decided to wait on doing anything until the next morning.

In spite of the fact that we went to bed late and I knew I had to get up early, I couldn't fall asleep. I tossed from side to side and imagined everything that could have happened while I initiated my lady companion in the mysticism of the East. In between tossing I lay quietly listening to my wife's heavy regular breathing, but she's not one to talk in her sleep, I was relegated to my own fantasies. Fifteen or twenty minutes it had been at the most, not any alarming amount of time, but how far couldn't such a clever, notorious charmer push it in twenty minutes while I in the course of the same time had nearly managed to convert my companion to Taoism. And the thing that bothered me the most: In what way could I reproach my wife with anything when I myself had delivered her into the custody of the beast?

My wife was comparatively hale and hearty after only four hours sleep, but I was feeling miserable and could barely get my morning coffee down.

»Did you have a good time yesterday?«

»Oh, yes,« she twittered. »I think it's been a long while since I had such a good time at a party.«

It must have been at that moment it happened. I felt something burst in my head, but I remained sitting very quietly, forced myself to drink yet another gulp of coffee, before I went on in a neutral voice:

»By the way, there's something I'd like to ask you about . . .«

»Just a moment, Honey, there's more coffee, we both could do with a real pick-me-up.«

She went out into the kitchen and got the coffee pot.

»How about you, did *you* enjoy yourself?« she asked while she poured my coffee.

I momentarily lifted my head, which rested heavily in my hands, and at the same time she looked at me.

»What is that?« she asked and looked anxiously at me.

»What?«

»Are you nervous?«

»What are you looking at?« I felt my forehead, my cheeks, tried to mirror myself in her red-rimmed eyes. She got a mirror, and now I saw it.

Just under my right eye there appeared at regular intervals of about ten seconds a distinct vibration which like a miniature flash of lightning spread over the upper part of my cheek and disappeared without a trace as suddenly as it came.

»You have a tic,« she exclaimed and ran around the table to me. She bent over me, put her arms lovingly around my neck and kissed the affected spot. »What are you nervous about, my darling, you over-exert yourself too much, you mustn't strain yourself so much. What was it you wanted to ask me about?«

»Oh, nothing,« I said. I was happy, proud, moved. Month-long exertions, meditations, hopes were crowned with luck. My wife immediately telephoned my employer and explained to him that my nerves were in such a bad state, probably because of over-exertion – – »You know yourself how conscientious my husband is about his work, to be completely frank: much too conscientious relative to the position and authority that the company offers him, not to mention the pay.« – – and that I had to have at least three day's leave, if I wasn't to end up with a total nervous breakdown.

Do I need to tell you that we have lived happily ever

since? Everyone shows me concern and respect, which strengthens my self-confidence, so that I'm able to behave and speak much more freely than before. People listen to what I say, people rely on what I say, people read my mood by my skin-gauge, count the intervals between each flickering spasm and from that take dead reckoning how they should further conduct themselves. My wife worships me and lets me sleep a great deal later in the morning. I got a raise and a promotion, indeed to a position of responsibility that involves my having to make many nervewracking decisions, but since that only involves holding my tics intact, I don't complain, or only outwardly.

But. For there is a but. In the beginning I could produce my nervous spasms when it suited my needs by simply beginning to speculate about what went on in that twenty minutes. Naturally I never questioned my wife about it, that would be like sawing off the branch on which I sat so well. But now there's a longer and longer interval between my tics. Up to now it hasn't brought any change in my job. I've done so well in my new position in the company that it would be unthinkable that I be transferred to an inferior job, and my wife is still just as solicitous about my welfare, although her solicitation no longer has the character of hysterical devotion. But what about the future? It's like getting hooked on drugs or alcohol, you have to get more and more to have the suitable effect. The thought of leaving her alone once more with the lecherous editor can still step up my tic-frequency, but I'm just a little over thirty, what won't I have to resort to in ten years when maybe that thought has long stopped agitating me?

I'm happy now. I've reached my goal, so I no longer have any goal. I lie awake at night thinking forward in time: My wife sold to an oil sheik's harem, I myself lying in constant convulsions foaming at the mouth.

I wake up tired and nervous in the morning. My wife looks at me:

»You still have a tic,« she says worried.

»Yes, what can one do about it? I wonder if there's anything that can be done about it?«

Hiccups

As far back as I can remember, I've enjoyed hiccuping, and my only regret is that I cannot bring the hiccups on in the way one evokes other pleasurable sensations. They choose their own day and time. To be sure they can arise in connection with rapid consumption of cold liquids, but don't think, then, that I can get them going by swilling cold water or beer. That usually only causes a sick stomach; hiccups can't be forced.

But when the miracle finally happens, I have to watch out. First of all I must be careful not to attract attention, and since hiccups almost always turn up when I'm at a party with many people, the situation is difficult, especially since the highest degree of enjoyment is to emit a real loud, uninhibited hiccup. So I try to hold it in first gear, and for the time being it just thumps a bit in my throat now and then or manifests itself through a sudden jerk of the head which can be camouflaged with ordinary nods or by tossing my hair back as if a fly were bothering me. Afterwards I may discreetly look around for a way out so that I can smuggle my hiccup out into the hall, into the garden or to the bathroom where it can finally sing out, but alas, only seldom do I get that far, for as a rule some sharp ear or eye has observed me: »Oh, you have the hiccups – – I can cure that.«

The cold water with which one usually starts the treatment isn't that bad. In the beginning I was nervous about it, but now I know that the hiccups are as little damaged by it as by vinegar with sugar in it and what ever else one comes up with as the never-failing remedy. I calmly drink these things, joylessly, in order to show my good intentions.

71

For I'd just as well not say that I should like to keep my hiccups; people think that I want to avoid imposing on them and find me only the more touching and helpless: »That is really admirable of you to pretend that it doesn't bother you, but we'll help you, just rely on us.«

Now come the hard tests: I stand on my head; I stand on one leg with a glass of water on my forehead; but I submit to everything in order to keep a good relationship with the other guests, and I do want to be invited again, not because the party interests me especially but because being together with many festively clad people puts me into that vibrant mood which constitutes such fertile ground for my hiccups.

Next I count backwards from fifty with my mouth full of water, and blushing I dry the drops of water off my jacket when, at twenty-four, a powerful hiccup blasts the water out of my mouth. But people smile encouragingly; the fact that I am a difficult case only increases the suspense. It would indeed be sad if the hiccups had capitulated already because of a sip of water; no, this is better than any party game. The gentlemen take off their jackets and heatedly debate what one now should resort to; the ladies rush in and out with pitchers full of splashing cold water; after a while the floor is a mess.

But at a certain moment it becomes quiet, everyone is looking at me silently with sparkling eyes. I move up against the wall and lose a hiccup for it is clear to me that they are going to scare me. That has, to be sure, never damaged my hiccups, and I really have nothing against people suddenly shouting »Boo« behind me, if only I don't know it beforehand. But the fact that I know it makes me nervous. From what direction will it come, what can they come up with, who is going to start? Frightened, I stare at them; indeed, I'll give a start in acknowledgement if they will only hurry up and get it over with.

But now they can see I am on my guard. There is a continued silence; to be heard are only my recurrent hiccups which I now let have free rein, at least to enjoy them to the fullest as long as I may. But I can see the worst is on its way. They all know there is one remedy which never fails, and one they have kept till the end, after everything else was unsuccessful. They look at each other – – who wants to take the initiative? There is no risk connected with it; the money is safe enough. Finally someone takes out his wallet, pulls out a ten-crown note and holds it up: One more hiccup, and it's yours. This is terrible. I try with all my might to hold the next hiccup down, in order not to offend anyone and not rob the man of this ten crowns which he does not dream of being in danger. I know it only makes things worse to hold back the hiccup, but what can I do aside from gaining time and hoping for a miracle – – that suddenly the doorbell will ring or a thunderstorm will break loose or there will happen something entirely different which can distract their attention. I press my tongue back into my throat like a cork with the result that the hiccup, when it finally comes, takes a running start all the way down from my kidneys and blasts itself a way out into the open with unbelievable power, so that I bang my head against the wall.

Everyone looks down into his coffee cup without moving or saying anything. For a moment the challenger stands paralyzed with his ten-crown note before flinging it over to me with a contemptuous air. And I am forced to take it. It isn't even of any use to say I am sorry; there is nothing to do. Everybody ignores me from now on. I can only wait for an opportunity to sneak out the door, downstairs and away, hiccuping sorrowfully.

After such an experience I keep to myself for a long time, but sooner or later my craving, not for company, but to hiccup, becomes so urgent that I again start to seek association with others and to ingratiate myself into social circles; now the question is to find some people who don't know me and my unfortunate inclination.

It is difficult in a smaller town constantly to reestablish a circle of acquaintances, I therefore have plans to move to the capital; there should be plenty of possibilities there.

Ice Occurrences in the Baltic

One evening I bumped into a group of old acquaintances in a bar in the city. One of them had been in America for a long time, and the others could have been, too, for that matter, because we hadn't run into each other for about a half dozen years. I got the different stories of their marriages and divorces and bankruptcies and the whole lot. In between they asked me: How are things with you, actually?

I hadn't been prepared to give an account of my intervening life that very evening, there was a good deal to take into consideration, so I began to think about working out my memoirs, all while I tried to the best of my ability to follow the further course of the conversation. But when I was about to close the last volume of the work, it had gotten so late that my various companions had to go home, and I was relieved, because I still found there were too many unexplained points in my life for me to be able to give a satisfactory presentation. To tell the truth, I was glad to have met them. If I bump into them again in a year, it's possible that I'll be able to give a better account. Certainly a great deal more may happen in a year's time, but then there's nothing else to do except be sure to keep up a little more with your life.

When I came to the trolley stop, a trolleycar pulled away right under my nose. I decided it was a red-letter day, it had been almost ten years since I'd seen them, I treated myself to a taxi.

The driver was young and new at the game, as far as I could see, but it was wonderfully warm in the car, I'd been freezing a little, it was sometime in March.

Shortly after heading out of town, he began to glance uneasily at me. I think he felt the time had come to say something. His Adam's apple bobbed up and down a few times, and then it tore out of him:

»It's cold today. I've just heard that big masses of ice are still floating around in the Baltic.«

Then he grew quiet and stared ahead with a single hasty side glance at me. What should I say? Here we sat in a wonderfully warm car far from the ice occurrences in the Baltic, which could easily have played a certain role by cooling the east wind and so contributing to lowering the temperature here on Godthaab Road, but first there was a west wind that day, as far as I remember, secondly I saw clearly that the climate wasn't at all on his mind, it was just important to him to be a little pleasant to his customers even though he had enough to do taking care of the wheel and watching out for red lights and thinking about where the address was.

I wanted to help him. Not because I thought it particularly meritorious to react to meaningless remarks, but on the other hand it was unlucky, too, that he should run into a tortoise like me as one of the first people he drove, maybe he'd begin to suffer from guilt feelings if he had driven a man from one place to another without exchanging a word with him, maybe he would seek out another occupation for which he had an even worse bent.

But to what he'd said I couldn't find anything to answer except, for example: »Yes, truly it's cold – – outside anyway, because in here it's wonderfully warm – –« or »You don't say? Are there still big ice masses in the Baltic, it was good you mentioned it, then we'll take a right here.« But neither of us would have gained anything by that.

I decided, then, to come out with something personal,

something I could vouch for, so when we drove over the viaduct, I said:

»I've just spent the evening with some of my old buddies from the technical school this evening.«

I would have said more, but he immediately brightened:

»How funny. – – It hasn't been very long since I was with a few of my old buddies, too.«

A little time went by in which neither of us said anything. I looked at him out of the corner of my eye. He was quite young. Even though his face was lean and he looked ahead intensely, his chin taut, there was still something soft and unfinished about him that made me warm in the midriff. He could have been my son. He had a pimple right where his cheekbone protruded, it wasn't ripe, the skin was red and tight around it.

There was something wrong with the business about the friends, and maybe I'd had so much to drink I couldn't really figure it out. In some way or other what we had said reminded me too much about the ice masses. I leaned back, gave myself plenty of time, this time I had to give it just the right turn so we could get a conversation going. Wasn't there something singular I could say about one of them, something that could contribute a little more than ice masses and coincidences. But if it's hard to say something about yourself, whom after all you've known a long while, it's harder still to have to get ahold of something definite about friends whom one hasn't seen for a long time. Maybe they've changed in the meantime – – from being lively, goodnatured fellows, maybe they've become bitter and cynical, such a thing could well be hidden during a single evening at a party with old friends. No, it had to be something that couldn't be misunderstood, something concrete, and suddenly it hit me: »One of my friends had lost all his teeth except for two or three,« I said, but realized immediately that that could seem offensive as if I wanted to make fun of my poor friend, which was far from my intent since I didn't have a stump left myself. I hastened to find something amusing, so I said: And one of them's just come home from America.

Then I took a deep breath and shut up.

But now it was as if he withdrew a little into himself, whether it was due to his having to watch the road or because he really didn't think his friends were a match for mine, as far as teeth and travels were concerned, so I added: »But the others had quite excellent teeth, aside from a filling here and there − − and I don't think most of them had been any further away that Jutland.«

I should mention that the driver didn't sound as if he were from Jutland, for then I would naturally have named a different locality. It was as if the atmosphere actually got a little better for a moment, he nodded to me with a slight understanding side-glance and began to keep watch again. On the other hand, it was as if we still hadn't gotten a step further, but had turned back to the ice masses in the Baltic.

Suddenly he stopped the car with a jolt.

»I hope you'll excuse me,« he said, close to tears. »I can see now that we've gone too far.«

»Oh, that doesn't matter a bit,« I said reassuringly.

He started to turn the taxi around: »I'll switch off the meter.«

»No, no,« I said eagerly. Actually, I did want to go a little farther, »just switch it on again, I've changed my mind, just drive on!«

He hesitated a little. »Where are we going then?«

»Just drive straight ahead,« I said, »I'll tell you when we're there.«

I shot a glance at the taxi meter and tried to figure out how much money I had on me, there was probably enough to go a good way yet.

We drove further through the suburbs and ended up on a half-finished concrete road which suddenly ran out, so we had to drive back and find our way to one of the more frequented main roads. I gave up thinking any more about old friends and began to look out the side window. It was almost nothing but fields now. A short distance in, a railway embankment followed us a ways, then it bent and disappeared, or maybe it was the road that bent from it. The fields were bare, cleared of stuff for conversation. Luckily the sky was only partly overcast so a touch of moonlight fell on the landscape, and a little later I caught sight of three white towers — — gas or oil tanks, but as we drove they were shifted for us, so that one slipped in back of the other two, and it looked like there were only two, and at the same time you might think that there could have been four or five standing in such a cunning relationship to each other that from the road you could only see two or three at a time — — you could drive by them every day in the belief that there were three at the most, while in reality there were many more.

It confused me a little, too, that I wasn't really sure whether there was gas or oil in them, or maybe kerosene, or perhaps a completely fourth something, e.g. vinegar — — you could end up making a complete ass of yourself, but on the other hand it should at least be possible to say something about them without going directly into the contents, e.g.: Such fellows as those must be able to hold a fantastic amount, I wonder if they're completely full? — — Anyway, it was better than ice masses, and then we could get things started at least. I was just about to say something along that line and had turned toward him when I discovered that he was also staring at them while silently moving his lips. Suppose he was about to say the same thing, I could have ruined it for him. I got quite sweaty at the thought.

He eased the speed to gain time. I looked at the meter, 13.40 − − 13.60 − − for now I could still cover it.

The road split in two. I couldn't see in which direction there was the most stuff, I suggested the left. I immediately realized my mistake, for the road was hilly and ran down into a hollow so there wasn't anything to see along the sides except now and then a tree looking startled as if our lights had wakened it, or a white gable gleaming a moment and immediately veering backwards into the dark. A moment later he had to slow down, a hare had come into the cone of light. It hopped from side to side, its white tail stump bobbed up and down, but every time we thought it would scurry into the rescuing and less travelled darkness, it sprang back again, as if it bumped into an invisible barrier, and tried the other side.

He slowed down even more. He was sweating, I could see, and no wonder, for the road began to go upward now. The road was humpy, and the motor sounded very offended.

»I'd like to stop here,« he said nervously, he didn't dare let go of the wheel and licked the sweat off his upper lip with his tongue − − »but I'm afraid it would be hard to get going again up over the hill, it's quite slippery here.«

I stared at the hare. It had slowed down, too, but still couldn't decide to scurry over to the side.

»Is it far now?« he asked.

»To where?« I asked stupidly, but hurried to add: »No, I don't think so.«

I looked at the meter − − 16.20, I had eighteen kroner on me.

»We'll be there in a moment,« I said.

We reached the top of the hill.

»Stop here,« I shouted. »You can turn around more easily here, I guess.«

He stopped and then looked at me, exhausted.

»Shall I turn around?«

The hare stopped a little ahead and sat down for a moment with his ears straight in the air. Suddenly it occurred to me that I had to pay for the trip back, too.

»You just turn around here, then I'll get out.«

The hare turned its face toward us for a second so that its eyes shone red. Only then it sprang into the darkness. It hit 16.60. I gave him my eighteen kroner and a few øre and got out. He poured the money into his change pouch, got in again and rolled down the window.

»Shall I wait for you here?« he asked.

»No, just drive on. Good night.«

I looked around, accustoming myself to the dark. There were trees on one side and black fields on the other. There were no lights or houses in sight.

He didn't start up, thought maybe I would change my mind.

»I'll walk back,« I said. »I've discovered that it's good for me to take a walk in the fresh air once in a while. You know, when you have sit-down work. – – But it's too far to walk both ways, you have to watch out for your sleep, too, so I like to take a taxi out in the blue, or black – – and then I walk home. It's very refreshing once your muscles have become accustomed to being upright. You should try it sometime. Well, naturally not now when you have the taxi.«

He still remained there.

»I think I'd rather walk during the day, if it were me,« he put in.

I was happy that he finally got his chance to say something, so I blurted out: »Yes, that's true, isn't it?« — — and hurried to continue: »I'd rather do that, too, there's so much more to look at, time flies by quickly, but unfortunately I don't have time during the day.«

»Oh,« he said.

I began walking. The road was really very muddy, but when I walked at the very side of the road, the heels of my shoes didn't stick in so often.

When I'd gone a little way, I heard him start up. He followed me slowly.

I began to whistle. Not because I thought he could hear me, but it can always be seen if a person's whistling, you have a different step and swing your arms as if you're in a great mood for hiking a long way.

Shortly after he pulled up beside me and rolled the window down.

»Don't you want to go back with me?«

»Oh no,« I laughed, »I've looked forward to this walk all evening.«

»I think it's beginning to rain,« he said and stuck his head halfway out.

I looked up. There were some clouds in the sky, the wind blew damply, but I couldn't see any sign of rain.

»To tell the truth, I don't have the money for the drive back. I always try to just have money enough for the drive out so I won't be tempted to ride home. Without a certain self-discipline I'd quickly slack off.«

»Oh, I see,« he said, disappointed and rolled up the window.

I trudged on, right now going downhill it went beautifully. He followed slowly.

When I'd gotten down to the main road and gone a good

ways, I looked behind me and discovered that he had vanished. I was a little sorry I hadn't gotten him going a little more, but, oh, well, since I didn't have the right to, it was probably better we parted.

I hiked right along now that I walked on asphalt. It was nice and easy at the start, but it wasn't long before the backs of my knees got tender. I tried to avoid straining them, that is bend my legs as little as possible and put my heels straight into the ground, but that didn't last long, soon it wasn't only the backs of my knees, but the shinbones and front thighs, too, that hurt. I discovered it really was time I needed exercise. Now I tried a new tactic: I sank at the knees at every tenth step so I could alternate between my muscles that way. But when I'd done that a half dozen times I found I couldn't straighten myself up from the bent position again. I had the greatest longing to sit down completely, but it really had begun to drizzle which was nice for I'd gotten hot. I unbuttoned my coat and put my scarf in my pocket, took a deep breath and gradually regained the feeling in my legs. Now I portioned my strength in another way, alternately hopping on my right and left leg. That went well for a while, I was about to hop around a big puddle and got a cramp in one of my legs, I forget which one now, and had to squat in order to not tip over into the puddle. I sat weighing the possibility of walking on my hands a ways when I saw light ahead. It was as if it relieved my cramp, I began to walk in a normal fashion toward the gleam of light and when I got closer saw that it came from a car parked on a side road. It was my taxi driver who had come by another way.

»How stupid I was,« he said. »You can just as well ride with me a ways, I have to go back there anyway.«

We drove toward town. The wheels sizzled in the rain.

Neither of us said a word, it was superfluous now. There were breaks in the rain where the moon peeked forth, or it could have been dawn, for it was early spring.

We passed these oil or vinegar tanks again. We both glanced at them without saying a word, I thought they were really very nice in the landscape and the rain, it was quite a pleasure to look at them without having to rack your brain about whether it was oil or varnish or cough syrup that was in them, or whether there were three or five. Incidentally, I think there were only three. I don't guarantee it. If anyone came out strongly for there being four or five, I could go along with it, more obstinate I'm not.

II

Friend of the Family

Erno has to go, things can't go on like this. As it is now, I jump every time I hear the doorbell, right away I think it's Erno, which it usually is, too. Several times a week he comes by and asks if he's disturbing us, always just at tea-time when I've come home from school. Why don't I simply say: You bet your sweet ass you are! and slam the door on his nose?

Previously Mona and I could take it into our heads to have an afternoon lay, in the summer exposed to the sun, warming our thighs, in the winter exposed to the wind, giving each other warmth, in the spring when spring simply flourished in us, but now? Now I don't dare engage in anything during the day for fear he'll suddenly ring the bell and interrupt.

If not slam the door, then at least indicate that his visit is inconvenient — — but on the contrary, I take his coat and briefcase right away and say: »It's good of you to drop by — — I think Mona is about to make tea so that's just fine, sit down, old buddy!«

Erno is tall and dark with hair that curls gently, plaintively at the edge of his neck, his smile is heartrendingly melancholy, particularly when he speaks of his musician's dreams, he plays the violin, has dreamed of playing at a nice restaurant — — who had any use for a violinist who could play only a single instrument, he asks resignedly. His father was himself a violinist, an Italian, so Erno's Danish has a soft, slightly shaggy accent which goes to your heart, I catch myself time after time sitting and listening to him openmouthed.

»I have to learn bass, tenorsaxophone, guitar, one has to be many-sided in our day, but what am I, one-sided, that wouldn't work out for me.«

His daily job is to stand in a music store selling electric guitars, trumpets, sets of drums and harmonicas, but nearly no violins. Thirty-five years old, owns three hundred and fifty records with every type of music: »Sometimes I'm surprised at how much music I can appreciate,« he says, »and how many different instruments, if they're played right, but as for myself I couldn't think of playing anything but the violin, and I haven't practiced now for a long time, it doesn't lead to anything, I'd rather listen to Oistrakh, that's enough for me for the moment.«

Mona comes in with her clinking tray, three cups, she has heard his voice from out in the kitchen. Erno has brought some records, which we have to hear right away, Ellington, Telemann, Yugoslavian folk music, Miriam Makeba, I get excited as usual and want to record them on tape right away – – don't you think we should, too, Mona?

I have stacks of reels, miles of tape of his lousy records, his wonderful records, I've never played a single one of them since, can't bring myself to touch them, hate the sight of brown plastic tape and the green magical eye that flickers nervously in time with the bass, I myself get a nervous twitching about my eyes, but I faithfully record it all on tape which I store away and never listen to.

I've asked Mona: »Aren't you a little sweet on him?«

»What nonsense,« she snaps. »I like Erno very much, but I have everything I want.«

»If I were a woman, I'd fall for him right away,« I say, »I don't understand you, you must have noticed his eyes when he listens to music, they get misty and vermouth-colored and squint a little, and he hums with a voice like warm wheatbuns . . .«

88

»Why do you think I married you?« she says brushing it aside.

She maintains that she has everything she wants, but she doesn't. The way her eyes hover about his, when she thinks he is completely absorbed in the music, the way her hands play with each other when he speaks to her, and especially when he doesn't speak to her, the way she puts her arm behind her head with a graceful, gossamer movement, rocking her dark, piled hair. – – I could throw myself on her on the spot if he wasn't there. But for me she never uses that attitude. Well, she has other excellent gestures in her repertoire which she doesn't employ when he is there, she pats her own arms, stretches her neck and pouts and fingers her nipples, it's wonderful and stimulating, but she has, to put it mildly, aspects that only he can bring out.

»Can you remember our trip to Norway when we were young lovers,« I say during tea, chrunching poppy seeds between my teeth – – the Gudbrands Valley, we cooled our tender hiking feet in an ice-cold mountain stream, I played for you on the harmonica, you stuffed your dress into your pants in order to get some sun on your thighs, there was just us, the mountains, and the sun, I carried both our knapsacks – – and the old woman in Stalheim, she apologized for only having one bed, fyra kroner, whether we would settle for it, we were delighted, made the hut rock and creak, fyra kroner . . .«

Erno became self-conscious and concentrated on the record, an Indian raga, but I keep on: »That time we swam naked on Thur Island, the poor man who wanted to take a walk along the beach but quickly turned around when he saw us, how hot it was that summer . . . . the phosphorescence . . . the haystacks . . .«

Mona smiles indulgently: »That's all very well, darling, but I wonder if that can be of much interest to Erno.«

Erno smiles sadly: »I love to hear about summer and freedom and happiness – – if I had my violin here, I would play an accompaniment ... but I've stopped playing, it doesn't lead anywhere, my fingers are stiff.«

He stares despondently at his long lithe fingers, which were born suntanned, Mona seizes his fingertips, bends them backwards so that he winces.

»You certainly have to keep on practicing,« she says sternly. »You're simply not to be allowed to let your abilities go to waste.«

»Do you think ... maybe you're right,« he mumbles distressed and pulls his long fingers even longer so they crack. Disgusting sound.

»But this summer we're going to Italy,« I say eagerly, »or to Greece – – or Ireland, think how much there is one hasn't seen, even in Europe, how will one manage to get to see everything he wants to, one life isn't enough ... .«

The taperecorder sputters and sparks, we'll have to wait for next time to record. I'm delighted, saves tape. On the other hand I'd really enjoy getting my hands on both his Vivaldi concert and the raga, on the other hand I know I would never listen to them again.

We drink rum with our tea, usually he has a few bottles down in his briefcase: »It's for you two, *my* stomach can't take it,« he says with a sad and courageous smile, he holds his hand over the glass when I want to pour, I never manage to get anything into him, only when Mona serves, simply pouring the liquid down between his outspread fingers, does he give in, move his hand with an apologetic smile and lingeringly lick his hand.

The sun suddenly comes out, we finish our drinks and go down to the canals, take a boat trip out to the harbor. It isn't really summer yet, not so warm as it looked from indoors, we have too few clothes on and sit close together,

Mona sits between us, opens her mouth to fill herself with all the fresh air she can bite off, while the woman speaker presents the Royal Dockyard, the mine sweeper, and the sand-pump dredger in three languages.

»Wonderful tongue you have,« I shout into Mona's ear. She sticks it completely out, and Erno leans forward to follow what's happening, she shows him her livelong tongue and laughs at his amazed expression, sticks her tongue out even farther at him. Now he takes up the joke and presents his improbably long, oval, scarlet-red, glistening tongue which stretches obscenely toward her tiny triangular, pink, slightly moist one – – they sit here a long time letting their tongues flutter like pennants in the wind to the great amusement of themselves and to the scandal of a heavily made-up woman on the bench in front, she continually turns appealingly toward me, but I stick out my tongue at her, my tongue is fat, crooked, coated, and warty as a toad's back, shocked she stares at it for a few seconds, blushes through her make-up, and says something to her husband, who also turns and looks sternly at my tongue.

We walk home along the Langelinje, Mona in her light green spring dress and white infinitessimally small sandals, with us in her arms.

»You're a sissy,« she says to Erno.

»No, I can't do without music, music is my life, but I'm tired of listening to myself play to empty walls.«

»You simply have to practice, then we'll record it on tape, but you must do something with it. Look, a chaffinch!«

We look, and sure enough, there's a chaffinch hopping along.

We sit under a red umbrella on the terrace of the Langelinie Pavillon and drink coffee. I keep my elbows close to the cup and my fingers gathered. I always manage to tip something or other over. Now I stare stiffly at all the objects that crowd together on the little table, cups, coffee pot, cream pitcher, sugar bowl, cookies, cognac glasses, ash-trays, I eye a passage between the cream pitcher and the coffee pot and carefully guide my right hand forward, secure a piece of sugar from the sugar bowl, make my hand narrow and salvage it safely back through the pass with the booty, which I don't let plop but sink into the coffee with a soft sizzle. It worked that time. I breathe a sigh of relief and stir with a slow regular motion, lay the teaspoon carefully down on the saucer, lift the coffee cup painstakingly to my lips with two particularly selected fingers, burn my lips, but don't lose my head, carefully put the cup down on the saucer again – – not out on the edge which I've done before – – now it is right in the center, stays there without my having spilled a drop of the black, scalding hot, slightly pitching liquid. Only sweating a little, I calmly reach down with my left hand into my pants pocket for my handker-chief while I keep on staring admonishingly at the coffee cup, get ahold of what I assume is the handkerchief, but which is in reality a corner of the tablecloth itself, go to dry my forehead with the supposed handkerchief, notice too late the counterweight, let go, but don't manage to spring aside from the sliding coffee pot and the avalanche of sugar and cookies, tip myself over with my chair, and cup and scalding hot coffee down on my stomach, lie on the gravel and kick with pain, cookies sprinkling down over me. The others each got their share. Erno cream on his trousers, Mona her coffee (with cream, but not sugar) over her light green dress. Some commotion develops. The waiter insists cooly but definitively on changing the tablecloth and the rest. We rub the stains with the napkins.

»One can't take you along anywhere,« Mona maintains.

In spite of my scalded stomach, which is probably fire-red

and disfigured with blisters, I rub away at Mona's spot and manage to rub it a great deal larger.

»Erno,« I say shortly after, »what you need is a change. I wonder why don't you ever take a trip to South America – – or even Central America? Or to a Folk High School?«

Erno cheers right up: »Oh, yes, why don't all three of us take a trip up to the skerries this summer – – I have half a motorboat with a friend – – I have it to myself at the end of July, and you have the whole summer off!«

The waiter comes with a new pot of coffee. This time I will do with losing my teaspoon down on the gravel. When I have bent down after it, I'm about to lift my head up under the tablecloth, but carefully get free and say:

»Erno, I mean it by God – – you know we think a lot of you, but wouldn't it be nice for all three of us if we didn't see each other for a while, think of all the things we could have to tell each other when we met again, cultivate some of your other friends and then let's meet again in half a year or two . . .«

Erno's eyes get large and dark as sunglasses, he folds up his napkin and pulls his chair out from the table, but Mona is already over with him and pushes him down in the chair again while she sends me a glance like a welding flame.

»That's an awful thing to say!«

He tries to get up but can't straighten his legs because of the chair and Mona's hand which pushes down on his shoulder, so he stands like that a while making half knee-bends.

My ice-cold fury is quickly melted, I realize that I can't follow through with it, above all I can't bear to see him this way. He isn't hurt, he's embarrassed and surprised, just wants to leave the wickedness of the world, home to his lonely violin. I leap over to him from the other side and with a joint effort we get him pushed down into the chair, which we shove in under him so that he's locked fast with his tie down in his coffee.

»Good grief Erno, pay no attention to my stupidities, I'm just trying to be funny in my own primitive way, you don't think for a moment that I was serious? Christ, you mustn't desert us!«

We get him somewhat more calmed down with more cognac. Mona presses my knee under the table, but at the same time squints somewhat reproachfully at me. The atmosphere is no longer the same, we have to go home and open up some bottles. I don't know which leg I should stand on to make it up. I bring the taperecorder to play some of the never-heard tapes, but, as mentioned, the recorder wasn't working.

Erno wakes for a moment from his gloom and tinkers with it, what can be wrong with it? I admit flatly that I have dropped it on the floor, I stumbled on the cord when I was trying to move it a few days ago, you know how clumsy I am, but I'll have it fixed for the next time you come!

»Next time,« he smiles joylessly, »I don't know . . .«

»Nonsense,« I shout and fill his glass − − »You're already too drunk to drive home, we can't in all decency let you drive home now. You can sleep here tonight on the sofa.«

»I wouldn't think of it,« he objects, but hiccups just then and remains sitting. »Besides I can't tolerate drinking at all,« he complains, ». . . my stomach . . .«

Mona is there with the evening snack, she has opened a can of crabs, and there was a left over bottle of schnappes in the refrigerator. I again put on the record he has brought, I'm delighted, finally progress of a kind!

Mona prepares the sofa for him, I support him while he's waiting to lie down, he pats my hair wearily before he falls down.

»No more violin,« he mumbles, »my stomach . . .«

»Just have a good sleep now, then play the violin for us in the morning,« Mona says and tucks him in.

I sleep in the next room, Mona in her room next to the kitchen.

I set the alarm, Erno has to get up an hour before me, but I don't want to miss seeing his face in the morning, their faces, read on them what has happened. What couldn't happen? One has to intervene, when they themselves can't figure it out. Finally finished with uncertainty, tomorrow I can pack my suitcase and gloomily announce: »I see I've made a mistake, it was I myself who needed to go away for a while – – goodbye, be good to her, Erno, she deserves it . . .« sniffle – –

Or I could look bitterly down into my coffee – – keep them on the pine bench for twenty minutes while I slowly stir, stir, and stir, finally rise, stand with my back toward the room and them and with my face turned toward the grey morning street, the exhausted morning people with their collars turned up around their pale harassed faces: »I will no longer put any pressure on you, Mona, but you will have to choose . . .«

Neither. Nor throw myself on my knees nor slam the door nor wave the bread knife. I would say: »One certainly can't blame me for being shaken and off-balance, but I like you both so much, so let's figure out an arrangement. Let's recognize the inadequacy of the monogamous marriage in the long run and the three of us get married quietly. We'll fix the tape recorder and play through all the old tapes, we'll take a vacation on Erno's half a boat, our children will have two good fathers and a healthy and loving mother . . .«

I open a mineral water I've taken to bed, take a gulp and push the bottle so far in under the bed that I won't knock it over if I have to get up during the night, give it a little nudge just to be sure and it tips over, pouring out its fizzing contents.

Probably nothing at all will happen: Nothing ever happens. If anything's happening, one never gets to know it anyway. And I notice that I'm not able to keep myself awake. I have to see about getting rid of Erno . . .

Mona stands in the doorway and has called me, three times she claims. It's not really light yet.

»Erno's sick, I've called for a doctor.«

I step out of bed, down into the puddle of mineral water, dry my feet off on the sheet and clump down in the puddle again.

»It's his stomach. Don't you think it's a crying shame to pour so much down him when his stomach can't stand it. Where has that doctor gone to . . .«

Erno lies doubled up in bed with his head all the way down between his knees. I feel his forehead, wet and cold. He has vomited blood and turns up the whites of his eyes. The doctor comes, takes one look at the patient, and immediately calls for an ambulance.

Mona asks me every day if I think he will die. I answer: I hope not. I mean it. If I lose him, I'll lose her, too. Possibly I can hold my own with the old living Erno, with the tape recorder as lightning rod, but I don't have a living chance against a dead friend of the family. I hope he recovers.

We take turns visiting him. On the way to the hospital I think about death among other things and realize that I've thought about death many times before. Particularly in the spring. I stop by an apple tree which foams with blossoms like a very slow wave. Earlier I could stand here gloating a little over my coming by here at just this moment, my thoughts turned to the dead and everything they missed.

But a little further along I see, perhaps, some earth that is turned so that old potatoes stick up in the sun. Suddenly there's something else. Maybe my time is coming before I suspect, in a moment in the middle of the crosswalk. It wouldn't surprise me. There's nothing else to do but make a detour. In this way I generally stay alive and get all around, even though certain appointments suffer. But I'll never be completely safe as long as I live.

Erno is better today. He sits up, angel-clad, pale and nearly cheerful under the teethgnashing curves of the diagram on the board. A rubber tube has snaked through his right nostril and down into his halved stomach, sucks the bloody discharge up into a brown plopping bottle. It's mate had bitten into a vein in his forearm and flushes nutrient fluids into his system, he is cheated out of the taste. He greets me nasally through this frogman's outfit so that new bubbles hatch in the bottles. I gasp for breath and grip the foot of the bed. His face has gotten so lean that his smile extends beyond its frame, his eyes bulge like mushrooms. Flickering images of concentration camp prisoners circle like vultures above me, I feel shamelessly well-nourished, duck and suck in my cheeks. Erno asks how things are at home. I ask for a glass of water. »I'm looking forward to eating with my mouth again,« he says nasally.

I clutch my throat.

»Say hello to Mona!« gurgles the brown bottle.

I stagger out. He waves cheerfully at me with his right snake.

Mona is glad to hear that he's doing well.

»You have to try to get him to play the violin again. He respects what you say. I would like to hear him play.«

I have to go in on the sofa and relax after the visit. I hope he recovers soon, my heart can't really take this. But I'm glad to be able to report he is getting better. Thank God. Soon everything will be as it was. The good old uncertainty that you can be sure of. But I'll have to get the tape recorder fixed for when he comes back.

The Phone Call

»You have to promise me, not a word to anyone,« said Frans. »They are for purely internal use. If the company found out that I'd taken them home with me, I'd be tossed out at once.«

Palle spread the pictures out in front of him, five six large photographs.

»Look, it's all here, from all possible angles. It's the police photographer who takes stuff like this and then our company makes inquiries, if it's a client that something's happened to, and asks for copies − − for insurance purposes, you understand. Sometimes there's a question whether it's suicide or accidental, there can be a great deal of money at stake. If it's premeditated suicide, there's no payment to the survivors. But there's no question here. We're just not allowed to show them.«

»No, there's no doubt here,« Palle admitted. The pictures showed a soldier who lay on a plank floor, probably in an Army barracks. He had taken his boot and sock off one foot − − only the one − − and had stuck a carbine in his mouth, pulled the trigger with his big toe and blown his brains out. Seen from the front, or more correctly, from above − − there wasn't anything remarkable except for a pool of blood by the side of his head, even his face was undamaged, very pale, nearly chalk-white, but maybe a flashlight was used. The eyes were rigid and wide open, the mouth half-open. In another picture, you saw the neck, or more correctly the gaping hole on one side of the back of the head. Just a dark crater with some wispy hair around it. In the third picture the brain lay in a little pool of blood, it was intact and looking quite like a brain. Palle was amazed that it was whole. In the fourth picture you saw the ceiling with bloodstains, and then there were a few pictures of the carbine and of the fragment of the cranium with sticky hair on it.

»If only it had been in color,« Frans said. »Agh, we have some that are much better. A man who strangled his five children while his wife was at work. The youngest was scarcely a year old. They were laid in a row. Jesus, it was something else. But I can't get ahold of them, it's too risky. Jesus, you should just see them – – these here are nothing.«

Palle looked for a long time at the pictures. He had never seen a dead person. He'd seen pictures of dead people, of course, but it could just as well have been someone who was sleeping or had fainted. But with the soldier there was no doubt: This man was dead, stone cold dead. It was the closest Palle had ever been to a dead person. He couldn't take his eyes off the pictures, and in order to gain time before Frans took them back again, he asked:

»Does anyone know why he did it?«

»I guess it was something about a girl who had broken off with him, or maybe she was going to have a child, I can't remember. Anyway, it had something to do with a girl.«

Palle laid his hand lightly over the picture, he still had to keep hold of it a little longer, try to imagine the soldier as living, with ordinary eyes, with a more closed mouth, smiling, looking, talking. It didn't work. The soldier wouldn't close his mouth, the eyes kept on staring rigidly. Strange that anyone could react so strongly, take his life so to heart that he died of it. Palle was simultaneously moved and envious.

The door opened and Birte came in, Frans hurriedly began shovelling the pictures down into his briefcase. Palle blushed.

»Well now, that's certainly something I'm not supposed to have seen, isn't it? Dirty pictures, my God, haven't you outgrown them? As if I hadn't seen things like that before. Can't you remember our honeymoon, Palle, when we proceeded according to the French postcards you'd gotten from your brother-in-law. It was the most tiring period in my life, and it irritated me that right in the middle of it all you incessantly had to consult the cards and see whether it was correct now, whether it was my right leg that should be up over your left ear or the reverse.«

Frans had quickly regained his composure: »Dear Birte, I truly believe I could teach you something new, but bear with a poor bachelor and amateur – – and now I have to withdraw.«

Birte showed him to the door.

»We're going to the movies. A war film, for a change.«

Palle didn't like the film. There was a welter of corpses, bombs, ruins, arms and legs, but that was all right for that matter if there hadn't been a speaker who unctuously advocated peace the whole time: Look how terrible war is, all of us must do our best to avoid a third world war, it would be even worse! In the beginning you swallowed it, but soon it was apparent that the peace message was a thin excuse for wallowing in blood, mud, misery.

However there were a few documentary sections, which Palle couldn't shake off afterwards. Some refugee faces, staring children, homeless dogs, a bathtub hanging out of a halved house. And particularly one from the German retreat in Italy. A group of young soldiers in a roadside ditch. They sat smoking during a pause in the allied bombing attack on the highways. You could see they were young, still their faces looked old. One of them stared right into the ca-

mera, as if he were thinking: Can't we at least be allowed to
rot in peace without being stared at?

They were home a little after eleven. At the foot of the
staircase they heard the telephone.

»I think it's ours,« Birte said.

»Who'd call us up this time of the night?«

Birte was already on her way up, her heels bobbed up
and down in front of him.

»It's more likely for her downstairs, she gets phone calls
at the strangest . . .«

Palle was about to lose his breath, he wanted to keep on
following those heels, they looked good after all the tanks.
One ate too much, was too well off. He came along behind,
the thick winter coat made him heavy, but now or never,
he took the last three steps at one time, slipped and went
down into a split, of which he would never have thought
himself capable.

Birte thoughtfully pretended she hadn't seen it, and he
was up again at once, stood behind her and filtered his
breathlessness out through his nose so that she wouldn't believe the few stairs had done him in. She rummaged in her
purse. It was still ringing in there, it *was* for them.

»Oof, I haven't got my keys with me − − give me yours.«

Palle was still not able to talk normally, silently handed
her the keys, but yet didn't let go of them and opened the
door himself.

As the door sprang open, the sound died away, and Palle
got a prickling feeling that the last deadline had run out. He
leaped into the room and tore off the receiver. Dial tone.

Birte turned on the light and turned up the heat again.

»Who could that possibly have been anyway,« she said.

She took off her coat and hung it up.

»Who it could possibly have been – – What do you mean by that – – it was someone by God!«

»It could have been a wrong number.«

Birte went into the kitchen and put the water on for tea.

Palle looked at the telephone dial. Guess – – guess, make your bet. DA – – FA – – ØB – – SØ – – and then the numbers. And all the fully automatic . . . Christ. He went out to Birte.

She was tapping the crisp bread with her nail to see if it was crisp enough.

»Well, maybe they'll call again,« she said.

»Who?«

»Whoever it was, if there was anyone.«

They drank their tea with just the table lamp lit.

»How do you like the caraway cheese?« she asked.

»Unsurpassed. Ask for it next time. What's it called? I mean if I'm the one to do the shopping?«

»You can't count on that anyway. I've had it all explained, it's not the name, it's something about the seasoning, it comes out quite differently every time.«

»Pure chance then?«

»You have to enjoy it while you have it, and hope it shows up again before your taste changes.«

»Well then, I won't change my taste any more from today on – – it's just the thing I want for the rest of my days.«

»Ten years ago you couldn't stand caraway cheese or seasoned cheese or any cheese at all, except the school cheese in a red rind.«

»Ten years ago I didn't understand a damn thing – – not even you.«

»Thanks a lot. Maybe you do now?«

»Maybe it's done you good to be seasoned a little, too.«

She kicked him on the shin, but it was with her slipper and painless.

»Not to mention your caraway taste,« he smiled and pulled his chair out in time − − »even though you can turn out differently from time to time, too . . .«

She sprang up, her eyes flashing lightning. It was probably an act, but you couldn't tell it from real lightning. He had burned himself a few times before, so he remained on guard.

She sat down again quietly. So it was just exhibition lightning. He wondered how she would look when she was completely beside herself so she couldn't even flash lightning . . .

She buttered a piece of crisp-bread for him. When he brought it up to his mouth it snapped in two, it was only held together by the butter and cheese.

»It wasn't intentional,« she said (excuse me didn't appear in her vocabulary), »I thought I had patched it carefully. Give it to me.«

But he had already laid the pieces together and bit crunchingly into them. The rattle of the diaphragm, Asta, Eva, Minerva.

»Are you still thinking about the telephone,« she asked.

»Well, maybe . . .«

»Who could it possibly have been?«

»You don't think there's anyone who cares to call us?«

»At this hour, I mean.«

»But frankly speaking,« Palle quickly finished his mouthful, »does anyone care to call us?«

»I think you're just tired.«

»Naturally people call us up. But seriously now . . . is there anyone who really cares about us, aside from just hearing how things are going, or to say they've bought a car, or that they're taking a little trip, or whether we've saved the paper from the seventeenth, for there was something there they wanted to see, and they've happened to throw theirs away.«

»What had you imagined? Should they pour out the story of their lives to you – – or ask for yours? What is it you expect, all in all?«

Palle bit into the folded up bread again. EXPECT – – expect. No, it wasn't like that . . .

»Why do you always leave a little in the bottom of the cup? It's the same with your milk at breakfast.«

»Excuse me, I've never thought about it.«

He hastened to drink the cold bitter dregs, while he smiled bravely at her. Ægir, Amager, Nora – – Amager, Poul . . . but why should it be him in particular?

She stood with her green slacks over her arm and the hanger in her mouth, she'd learned that from him. Marriage, habit or profit. The slacks were hanging down so he couldn't see her from the front, but in a moment she'd turn and go in. He swung around in the chair so as not to miss the sight, threw one leg over the arm of the chair.

»It could have been my mother,« he tossed out, »maybe something's wrong with Dad.«

»So call her up,« she said as she turned her back to him. He sat so low that he could both see where her thighs met and sense where they parted again below her buttocks.

»Not at this time of night.«

»But she can call you?«

»Well, no one's saying that it had to have been her.«

»Do as you like, I'm going to bed now anyway.«

She hung the hanger with the trousers in the built-in closet, went over and turned down the heat, and went into the other room to fuss with the sofa bed.

Palle sat up straight in the chair again. If there was something wrong with his father, there was nothing he could do about it anyway, and then besides he'd find out about it in the morning. He turned up the heat again a little. Remember to turn it down. Buttoned up his shirt and sat back.

Suddenly it struck him that if he phoned, there could be someone else phoning him at the same time. He was tied hand and foot. He sat up with a jolt and began biting his nails. If he was going to call, it had to be soon, it was after twelve, one couldn't in all decency . . . there was nothing to do but take the chance. No, he'd give the telephone a chance first, five . . . no, four minutes: if it didn't ring again within four minutes, he would call someone or other and then hope for a bite, or at least not be called himself meanwhile. He began on the nails on his left hand while he watched the clock.

When the four minutes were up, he dialed AM and gave the number. A long time passed. College prep course, excursion to the morain formations in the Deer Park, where Poul failed to appear; he had dropped out the day before, and the teacher's comments beneath the beech tree: »He was congenial and charming as a person, but was unfit for scientific work. This has been an obituary and it was well-meant.«

Early untidy spring some place on North Falster, everything had gone to hell, but they took a walk in hell together, Poul failed some entrance exam or other and he himself frightened out here in the province by Birte's plans to take a job in a home in England or France before they got married. Poul and he walked slowly along the beach and caught sight of a fishing stake that had washed up on the beach. With a joint effort, they got it afloat nicely and gave it a shove outwards. Poul stumbled and fell headlong in the shallow water, but remained lying completely still and soaked until the pole turned out into the current and went east.

»At last,« said Poul then, »that was wonderful, by God.«

And Palle remembered the relief he had felt at the other's relief, from now on everything would inevitably go better. And things had gone very well for him, too, but for Poul?

Finally he heard a voice: »Hah?«

»Yes, is it you Poul, it's Palle – – Jesus, please excuse me for calling at this crazy hour – – had you gone to bed? Oh, that's too bad – – no, it was only – – someone telephoned me, but I don't know who it was.«

»Didn't you ask who it was?« came the sleepdrowned reply from Poul.

»Yes, of course – – that is, no – – you see . . . I didn't talk to the person in question at all – –«

»Did either of you say anything?«

»The thing is, the telephone rang just as we were on our way up the stairs, so I didn't get . . .«

A strange hollow sound came out of the telephone, the poor man was obviously in his bare feet, freezing. Palle hastened to finish his explanation:

»And so I thought it might have been you, but I can see that it wasn't, please excuse me, but if it had been something important, you see – – well, good night, Poul – – and . . . hey, Poul? Are you still there – – won't you stop by someday, it's been a long time . . .«

»Oh, yes,« there came despairingly.

»But we can give you a call about that, now hurry back to bed again, and excuse me for waking you this way. Give our regards . . .«

Palle stood listening a little while without hearing the click.

»Good night, Poul, hurry in now to . . . oh . . . be sure to get in under the quilts.«

He heard a shiver: »Heww – – huhh – – good night . . .«

Finally the click came.

Palle slapped the receiver back and stared at the telephone. Not a sound. He looked at his watch, nearly three minutes. There could well have been a call in the meantime.

»You're not sitting there calling up people at this time of night?« Birte stood in her pink pajamas with toothpaste foam at the corners of her mouth.

»I've been thinking over what you said. You're right, actually, who should ever conceivably call us, really, at all? It's always we who call them, isn't it? Does anyone ever call, on their own?«

»You're tired. Come on to bed.«

»You're the one who's tired.« Palle straightened up. »Anyway, I can't go to sleep before I've figured this out.«

Birte pulled her chair over in front of him and sat down with her bare toes on his thigh.

»What is it you want to figure out, then?«

»What friends we have anymore, real friends, people who . . . who would really be distressed if we got sick or . . . went away for a long time.«

»Why don't you think about whether there's anyone we'd be distressed to see leave?«

»It's always us who call.«

»Yes, but then what do we call about – – do we *really* call as you say, don't we just call and arrange something, too, are we seriously concerned about their welfare on the phone, do we confide . . . I don't know what it is you want people to use the telephone for, there are things, after all, people have to talk about *without it* – – sit and chat together in the same room.«

»Good, but then what do we talk about when we're in the same room – – work, children, troubles, politics, books, the future . . .«

»Good gracious, isn't that more than enough? What else do you expect?«

Expect – – expect, back to that again. It wasn't something that could be defined in a word or two, and if one finally found a word for it, at the same time it meant something entirely different which didn't have anything to do with the matter. Friendship, contact, intellectual rewards, oh Jesus, all of it was the kind of stuff that was in the pamphlets and church magazines that came in through the mail slot certain days of the week and which they'd pounced upon when they first got the apartment because it was something for *them* that had come to their residence, someone had ferreted out that they were living here and actually sent something to them – – but now they tossed it unread into the wastebasket.

»You should unbutton your jacket when you sit in the easy chair. You get such ugly folds across your stomach one would think you had a car.«

Birte tried to unbutton the jacket with her toes. Palle took it off and threw it across a chair, it happened to hang crooked, looked like a scarecrow with broken arms.

»I could understand if we had moved in from the country,« Palle continued, »but we were born here in the city. We have known a lot of people. I must have played with a dozen children before I went to school, have attended classes with, let me see . . . twenty some in grammar school – – yes, all in all half a hundred. To that add the college prep course, twenty, thirty others, and then later on – – but where the hell have they gone – – who's left?«

»We do have each other. Aren't we left?«

Birte tickled him in the side with her toes, but he had no desire to laugh now, and so it only hurt.

»Who could it have been.«

Palle went at the remains of his fingernails.

She got up without answering, rocked up on the balls of her feet a few times for her flatfootedness. Then she went to bed.

Palle turned slowly to the phone. Dumb and shapeless it looked, the receiver hung down over each side as if the whole thing had melted together. There was something more vigilant about the first telephones where the receiver hung on one side and you had to turn a starting crank as if you were winding up the imminent conversation. Plant the short receiver in your ear instead of settling your head against this wheedling bakelite sausage.

He took a piece of paper and began writing names down. Hans, Ellinor, Thygesen, Onkel, Janus. Sat a while staring at the names. They made no sense to him. It was like a rote list of words he had learned, durch für gegen ohne wider um . . . he'd forgotten how they should be used, what they governed. On with it, there had to be more lists, someplace or other there had to be a hole – – Kristensen, Markussen, Christensen with Ch, did he know anyone by that name or anyone with Kr, he sat weaving random names in, the hell with it, on, better systematically, alphabetically: A, Abel, Asger, Arild – – that was the one with time, Arild's time – – Bent, Bitten, Børge, Balle, . . . Balle. Could that be possible. Balle, he was the one who didn't like to ask for the return of a loan if it was under ten kroner, as they cunningly figured out and so they always borrowed five or seven seventy-five and amounts like that until one day some idiot tried to put him on and asked to borrow 9.99. From that time on he never lent anything less than ten kroner and began to keep accounts, too. – – Balle with the runaway sandwich maid, who drank up his money, and cheated on him with others. Should I marry her, Palle, I think she needs a fixed point in her life (balling point, thought Palle), a home, then she'd stop with the others, don't you think I should jump into it, damn, I think I'll do it! That's the way Balle could take it into his head to call him in the middle of the night, maybe it had been precisely him, he probably hadn't finally decided yet.

Palle dialed the number, then happened to think that Balle had probably gone to Greenland, it had been five years since they'd spoken together, they were probably complete strangers to each other, really he had no desire to talk with Balle. Did he want to talk with anyone at all? Was it he himself there was something wrong with?

He put down the receiver. He wished he could call the soldier without the neck and ask how things were with him during the last hours before he took his shoe and sock off. Or talk with the young soldier with the old face and the hopeless look in the roadside ditch, ask what he had seen, and whether he had later come to look on existence differently.

He went to bed. He felt that she lay awake beside him, but didn't take any notice. He couldn't sleep. They both lay there awake.

Then the telephone rang.

»Aren't you going to get it?« she asked.

Palle didn't answer. His whole body was stiff as a board.

»Are you asleep?« Birte touched his arm — — »What's wrong with you? You're shaking. Is there something wrong?«

»It must be a wrong number. Someone we don't know. At this time of night.«

»Would you rather I answered it?« She tried to get up, suddenly he could move, he took her in his arms.

»Just stay here.«

She lay down again. He could feel that she lay looking at him.

»What is it like to die,« he said.

»Why do you ask about that,« she answered after a long pause.

»I want to know. Do you ever think about death?«

»No. Only when it's someone in the family that dies. It's been a long time. But I myself tried to die once for that matter . . . that was a long time ago, too.«

»I never heard that.«

»I never told anyone about it. When we were in Norway. You remember that I sprained my foot when I ran into a boulder?«

»Yes.«

»Actually, I died.«

Birte lay on her back looking up at the ceiling.

»You remember, I skied down ahead, I was to warn the rest of you when there were any dangerous turns or drops, because I was already familiar with the ski run. I really wasn't worth a tinker's damn because it had been a year since I'd tried it, and everything looked different, the snow cover was hard as glass. And then what I feared came, a slope so steep and long that I realized you others wouldn't escape unhurt. If I'd been alone I probably would have taken it, but then I just managed to turn off. I was going so fast that I couldn't brake quickly enough and I steered right toward a huge, snowcovered boulder. I didn't even have time to react, I barely had time to think: Now you'll die, be smashed against the stone, never get to warn Palle and the others. Then there came a flash of fire, dazzling snow or sun.

I'd probably been lying unconscious with open eyes for a long time. I lay and saw only: my ski boots, the skis, some thin branches and an inconceivably blue sky. I lay for a long time, looking without thinking about what I saw. It was the strongest thing I've ever experienced, but I didn't think about that until later, I just lay there and was there, looked, lay, without thoughts, without a soul, totally empty. It was only later that the question popped up: Why is the sky where the earth should be, why are there branches and blue sky between my skiis, where has the earth gone, how did I get here.

I had flown through the rock by a miracle. I had after all myself seen how I steered right into it, and now I lay on my back with my skiis up in some branch thicket. In some way or other death had opened itself ajar for me and let me slip out on the other side. What I now lay looking at was something I shouldn't have seen. If it had happened right, I should have stopped seeing the instant I was smashed against the boulder. Everything here was something I shouldn't have experienced at all, everything that happened from now on was something extra, gifts, a bargain.

With great difficulty I freed my feet from the bindings and got up on my feet. It turned out that the boulder had been covered with a huge, sloping snow-pillow. The skiis had actually only brushed the side of the boulder and tore through the snow-pillow which I thought was the upper part of the boulder. I'd only hurt my left ankle. The whole thing had probably only taken four minutes. So I hurried over to the trail and called to you, and heard you answer from above, »We're coming!« It was as if your voice struck me in the stomach, I doubled over and pressed both hands against my navel. I burst into tears and wet my pants. It's the shock, I said all the while to myself. Straighten up now, Palle's alive, you're just in shock. How good it was that you were the first one to reach me. I was very fond of you back then, but from that moment it was something completely different. You were the first person.«

»And now?«

Birte turned over on her side and laid one leg over his.

»It's strange you made me remember it. I haven't thought about it for a long time. I never thought that I'd forget it. I believed fully and completely that every moment in the whole future would become a gift, I would never ask for anything. But one forgets how it is to die. One forgets how much you love each other. You mustn't think it's gone − − I only forget it because of so much else, I'm sorry about it. But it's just like it comes back when one speaks of it. Otherwise I wouldn't have spoken of it. How did you get me to speak of it?«

Palle seized her with all fours.

The Drowning Man

Villy sat up in bed. His heart beat a little too fast, he must have lain on the wrong side. It was light enough to see his watch, nearly four. He who hardly ever woke at night. One doesn't remain robust and twenty-five, does one? A pretty story, perhaps the preface to a long series of heartbeat nights.

He got up in several stages, first on end, then swing the legs out onto the floor, then up and stand, but now his heart had calmed. He went over to the window and looked out. The rose-hip thicket on the beach below the house looked completely black, but everything else was a fine silver gray with soft furry contours, the summer cottages, the flag poles, the dunes, farther away the beach hotel with its tower sticking up like a short fat thumb. The opposite coast was hidden by a light mist – – usually there were a few faint lights out there, smouldering. On the other hand the water was visible far out, dark and motionless, even though he heard the brief rhythmic slaps of waves on the beach, followed by the fizzing backsplash which made him involuntarily curl his toes on the wooden floor so as not to be sucked out with it. Not wise to stand too long in bare feet, it was probably not only your heart you had to watch out for in the future. He was about to mosey back to bed when an irregularity on the surface of the water caught his eye. Something that was darker than the surrounding dark, but got lighter now and then as it changed position. He squinted, could it be a person? It might well be a person's head and a pair of shoulders, but it was quite a way out, it must be a night bather who was tougher than the average. And alone, too, at this hour. An arm came up, there was no doubt about it, he could almost see the water dripping from it. But now the other arm came up, too, what could that mean? Distress, cramps? or simply a moment's gaiety while he was treading water? Now the arms sank again. The phenomenon didn't come any nearer, but had perhaps moved slightly to the left. And now first one arm and then the other reached up again and stiffened in that position . . .

His feet got cold and he hurried over to the bed and stuck them into his slippers, but before he had gotten them really on he heard a single, ghastly sound, a brief bark, almost like that of a seal. He feverishly pushed on one of his slippers, his big toe had gotten snagged on a thread and wouldn't go in, he flayed the slipper off again, but the thread cut into his toe and he swore aloud. Finally he got the thread snapped with his hands, got the slipper on right and hurried over to the window. The ocean was completely still and smooth. The night bather, or whatever it was, had vanished.

Villy remained standing a little while staring disappointedly at the spot where he had observed the sight. Then suddenly he thought of the drift – – toward the left it had to be – – and shifted his glance toward the spot about where the night bather ought to be. Panic gripped him at the thought that the man possibly had glided farther and farther west while he himself was standing in the same place, had thought it was enough to stare straight ahead. He rushed to the chair where his pants hung and got them on quickly. The man could be yanked under a second before Villy managed to sight on the right spot.

While he was on his way toward the nearest houses, which all lay in darkness, he tried to remember who had moved up here and who hadn't. He stopped a moment. What did he really have in mind? To call for help? Before

116

people realized what was wrong, several precious minutes would have passed, and then what could they do? And who might have a telephone, he knew them only fleetingly, kept to himself because he wasn't here on a vacation, pre-vacation one might call it, in order to do some accounts he couldn't find peace for in the city. But even if he was lucky enough to happen on someone who had a telephone, what good would it do, at least another quarter of an hour would go by before you could get ahold of those whose job it was to row out and save people, yes, close to a half hour, and by then it would be too late.

Instead Villy ran along the little path through the rose-hip thickets down to the beach, but then stopped again, for if he swam out himself looking for the drowning person, wouldn't it be better before going to let others know so they could get help? Suppose he found the man but didn't have the strength to rescue him – – his swimming was only so-so, strictly aside from the fact that he would put himself in mortal danger by venturing so far out, and then his heart began to pound again. He swore and turned around, and in his confusion he ran in among the rose-hip bushes and got caught on the thorns several times, at last hopelessly. Either he had to tear his pajama top or he had to begin freeing himself thorn by thorn, and even though the first choice, given the seriousness of the situation, was the only right one, and he didn't have any patience at all for the second, he chose to coax his way free and get his fingers full of thorns, for how would people react to a man in torn pajamas who woke them up a little after four shouting that someone was about to drown? They would either sniff his breath or stare out at the water and ask: Where? And no matter how much he insisted he'd seen it with his own eyes, he couldn't expect them to give him their confidence when they hadn't had the opportunity of getting to know him and

forming a basis for trusting his word and his sound judge-
ment.

It occurred to Villy that the pre-requisite for rapid help
was that he had to approach the other summer residents,
talk with them when he walked by on the path, praise their
plants, offer to pick up their papers if he was going to the
station anyhow, ask them their advice about growing let-
tuce, for example, but he had neglected all that, and it
would take at least a week to establish enough neighborli-
ness, he was, in other words, not a quater of an hour but a
week too late for it, and hysterical at the thought he tore his
pajamas free from the thorns in a single yank, but strangely
enough they weren't torn at all, the arm lost its shape a
little, but he couldn't see any tears in it.

He ran as hard as he could down to the edge of the
water, but now another problem presented itself. Up from
the cottage he had had a fairly good bearing, nearly a
straight line, but what about here where his course has shifted in relation to the other two measuring points, the window and the person's probable point of disappearance? Villy turned and looked up toward his window, but it was no
help to have just one bearing, and besides he was now so
much lower that he couldn't survey as much of the sea's
surface as he had from above. He began to run to the left
down along the beach, but how far had the unfortunate
person been carried? Good lord, what about these currents
and undercurrents besides − − as long as the fellow was in
sight, he was carried to the left, but what if he had sunk
now to a calmer level − − or on the contrary had been
taken by an outgoing current, the water was treacherous
here as soon as you got out beyond the first sand bar.

If only the idiot had called for help at once, then there
would have been no doubt about the direction, almost a
straight line. However, he hadn't called for help at all, just

let out a kind of bark, how much weight could you give to that? After all, it could have been a person who wanted to take his own life, but at the last moment was about to scream which he succeeded in suppressing to a yelp, and then the situation was entirely different. Naturally you shouldn't let a suicide carry out his confused project as a matter of course, still there was a certain sense in not putting your life at stake – – if you could only be sure it was a suicide. But suppose it wasn't he himself who had choked the scream, maybe he had gone under and gotten a mouthful of water. Villy took another step, slid into something cold and slimey and let out a gasp. It was a jellyfish that had flopped up onto the beach. He wiped off his slipper in the sand and looked at his watch. He had his watch on, it was an encouragement and comfort to him to realize that at least he'd been ready to rush out into the waves without thinking about his expensive watch. No mean consideration. But it was half past four, it would be hopeless now.

He was dead tired, but his heart pounded, and he knew it would be impossible to fall asleep now. But the next time he looked at his watch it was half past seven, so he must have dozed.

The sun's rays slanted through the window and hit the upper part of his trousers, which hung over the chair, slack and crumpled. He thrust a hand down and got his slippers, let a finger run across the smooth, black-worn soles, a little sand sprinkled down on his breast, but what did that prove, he often walked around outside in his slippers. The events of the night were painfully clear to him, but his confusion and doubt on the beach now appeared to him so incompatible with his usual domestic peace and compsure that it seemed like a dream situation, the same feeling of powerlessness and disintegration which recurred in his dreams. He examined his pajama sleeve, which should have been

119

damaged by the thorns, but it was unharmed except for a few tiny irregularities in the weave, possibly a result of the thorns pulling the threads from each other without breaking them. Just to be sure, he went over both sleeves and the rest of his pajamas. Only way down at the bottom of one trouser leg was there a thread that stuck out in the air, but theoretically that could have been torn by a splinter in the doorframe. He got up and examined his pants, there was nothing unusual.

He went over and positioned himself with his bare feet on the warm square the sun had baked on the floor. Then went over and laid his arms on the windowsill. It scorched the thin skin of his underarms, but he forced them down against the red-hot wooden sill and soon after it just felt comfortable. In the path in front of the rose-hip thicket people in bathrobes went for their morning papers. The early bathers had been going long since, gasping they called to each other while they gingerly picked their way across the stretch of stones. One of them had just reached the sand bottom, turned now toward shore, stretched his arms over his head and let himself fall backwards with an ecstatic bellow. That was not the way the arms last night were stretched in the air, and yet, it had been dark, and farther out, he could have been mistaken. It was not beyond the realm of possibility that it was precisely one of these robust early swimmers who had wakened in the night just like himself from being too hot, or simply because his sleep came to an end, so he had to go out and refresh himself and acquire a little healthy fatigue so he could sleep once more. And while Villy had struggled to put on his slippers, the fool must have had enough, had swum a little to the right where Villy hadn't thought to look at all and had waded ashore beyond Villy's narrow range of vision.

120

Farther down the beach in front of the hotel and the cabins there were already numerous people, the sun was strong. Many of them had brought beach chairs, but hesitated to set them up, the wind was somewhat stronger down on the beach than in the lee of the hotel and the houses. The bathing flag pointed inland, it was the green one, good bathing conditions then.

He got one of his slippers from under the bed, stuck his hand in it. There were some loose threads in the worn flannel lining, but it could be from wear, only the eye could decide that, and that meant that he could have to cut the slipper up in order to get at the place, but the more the beach filled up with cheerful, noisy life, the more unreal the night's experience seemed to him, and besides, he liked the slippers.

After an absent-minded breakfast he got a plastic bag from the pantry and went down to the rose-hip thicket. First looked for footprints in the sand, but there was an abundance of them, footprints in all directions. He didn't care to be looking around off the path without a credible purpose, so he pretended to be picking rose-hips, while he actually looked for a little white thread that matched the one that was torn from his pajamas, but the thicket looked entirely different in the daylight.

When someone came by on the path, he immediately set to work picking rose-hips and swung the plastic bag demonstratively, presumed to say »Good morning« to a man he thought he had seen before, who knows, maybe it could be the beginning of the acquaintances he had had such need for last night. But when he finally gave up the search, he had only a half dozen rose-hips and no thread.

He took the bag up and then immediately afterwards went down to the beach. Down by the bathing cabins the

attendant was watching some young girls who were fighting over an air mattress a little way out. He was sturdy,
going-on-flabby and already dark brown. Villy had never
seen him in the water, but it probably wasn't possible to
keep watch on the beach and swim at the same time.

»Well, there's not much danger of drownings today, is
there?« Villy said. There was a spasm in the dark brown
back, the man turned briefly toward Villy and then kept
watch again, this time in a different direction.

»Do people sometimes get into trouble here?« Villy continued.

»So they say,« the man said sullenly. »Nothing much has
happened in my time.«

Maybe he did his swimming at night, it could have been
him Villy saw during the night.

»But I suppose at night there's no attendant, people
sometimes go swimming by moonlight, I guess – – isn't that
dangerous?«

The attendant shrugged his shoulders. Villy thought that
he was taking time for a well thought out answer, but when
a few minutes had gone by he realized that the shrug was
the answer.

Villy offered him a cigarette, but the attendant just shook
his head and kept his eyes on the waves.

»Suppose someone drowned last night, where would he
be washed ashore?«

The attendant winced as if someone had puffed smoke
into his eyes. Then he waved his head wearily up the beach.

»Over by the lighthouse.«

Villy turned a moment toward the white tower at the
end of the bay. When he looked back, the attendant was on
his way over to the cabins.

After Villy had eaten lunch, he wrote a letter to his wife
in which he asked her to wait a few days before coming be-

cause the accounts were giving him trouble and he had to have complete peace and quiet.

He'd always had the principle of keeping his ears closed to casual gossip, hurried through town neither looking left nor right, and only relaxed when he was alone in order not to intercept remarks which weren't meant for his ears anyway but could lead him into fruitless and time-wasting conjectures. But today he forced himself to walk slowly and keep an ear out for all the local topics, which primarily had to do with speedboat terror and the fantastic plaice you could buy down at the harbor, not a word about drowned or missing persons. He bought one of the fantastic plaice and walked quickly home.

The remark about the troublesome accounts had first and foremost been directed at himself, he hoped thereby to be able to shore up his guilty conscience so much that he would simply have to finish the accounts quickly. But when he sat down at the cottage with the pile before him, it was impossible to concentrate. It was also much too hot. Late in the afternoon he left it all lying there and went for a walk toward the lighthouse.

He walked by the water's edge in his bare feet and stepped around the jellyfish that lay there at short intervals. Just before the lighthouse there was a stretch with piles of seaweed. The surface was bone dry and redhot from the sun. It was a pleasant and chilling feeling to walk on the brittle, springy, warm mat and once in a while feel your heel or a few toes slide down into the ice-cold and slimey underside; he had tried it as a boy.

After the piles of seaweed there was a small inlet where refuge and garbage drifted in and got hung up. Egg cartons, plastic bottles, a wicker basket, small boards. He fished up a piece of board, it was oblong, pale, and polished, with deep furrows where the soft wood was eaten away. It could almost have resembled a large foot with a partly gnawed off big toe, the other toes missing. The lapping of the waves dissolved the sand under the balls of his feet like sugar. He sank deeper and deeper, remembered the feeling from his childhood years, too, the dread of quicksand, curled his toes to keep a little to stand on, a footfull. Suddenly a bigger ripple came in and sucked the bottom out from under him so that he was about to give way. He flailed his arms and dropped the wooden foot into the water, fell on his rear, came up with a gasp and began to run home. When he ran over the piles of seaweed, his feet slapped through the crust at each step and deep into the cold mush.

At home he changed his pants, put on shoes and hurried into town. It was a quarter to six, the telegraph office had just closed, but he knocked so long on the frosted window that the man thought it was a matter of life and death and let him send his telegram:

»Cancel letter. Take first train up.«

When he got home again, he made himself blind and deaf to everything and threw himself into the accounts. When he finally had to eat something, it was half past nine and by then he had gotten more done than all the previous week, but he had little idea of how it came about, automatically, unconsciously.

He put the pan on the gas stove and threw the plaice in it, couldn't even wait until it was properly fried, ate it half raw, hot and crisp on the outside, cold and odd on the inside, delicious, refreshing. The bones that had always irritated him he didn't notice today, spat the worst of them out the window, swallowed most of them and fell asleep with the rest of them bristling between his front teeth.

When he woke it was four o'clock. He knew it without looking at his watch. His heart beat fast, but he didn't find that disturbing, had almost counted on it. He got up at once and went to the window. The thicket lay there like a huge black sponge sucking the worst of the darkness into itself. The sand, the dunes and the houses were luminous gray, the sea was calm with a mellow graybrown color, everything was just like last night, and he breathed deeply in the cool night air. It was like waking after a confused dream of a sullen attendant, a closed telegraph office, unimportant accounts, a plastic bag with rose-hips, freshly caught giant plaice. It was *now* he was awake, he felt it in every breath that sent a cold chill down into his lungs, what further proof need he have? And of course he had been awake the night before, too, the drowning person's cut-off bark still sounded so lifelike in his ears, as if the sound had only died away a second ago. Involuntarily his eyes sought out the spot where he had last seen the man when he stretched his arms in the air. Villy tried to lift his arms in the same stiff manner. Dropped them hurriedly, but stretched them up again shortly after. He stood like that a long while looking out into the dark where there wasn't a soul who saw him or was interested in him. He was already getting training in knowing the difference between this really very simple condition and the everyday one where he assumed he was awake, but basically wasn't there, spoke and acted as if he had temporarily travelled out of his good skin and had hired someone who looked like him to take care of the current business until he came back, but for God's sake let the important business wait.

Now he had returned, stood in his own flesh and blood with goosebumps on his arms, but what about tomorrow, what about the other days? Would he gradually learn to take action during the brief moments when you wake with a shock, as he did this afternoon when he did the only right thing, the thing he had fumbled around for all day without suspecting that it was that he was searching for, that thing that had to be done ... He had nosed around for a torn thread, believed it was a matter of getting into his neighbor's good graces and getting to the bottom of his accounts, and then, in a brief flash, when the sandy bottom gave way and twitching he fell on his rear, it became clear to him that he should send for her. Tove, his wife, where had she gone? Granted, she was still there, out on the edges, in the background, smoothed pillows, was herself a pillow to fall back on, but once hot so many years ago she was in the center, and he could circle around her, saw her from all sides, looked at her when she was there, and saw her before him when she wasn't there. It was there he should be again.

His arms prickled, he let them sink and noticed the arteries on the back of his hand swell up burning. He put his slippers on and went outside. The neighboring cottage blocked the lighthouse so he could only catch the gleams out over the water without being able to eye their source. Through his thin sole he felt a stone, picked it up to throw it down on the beach to give a sign of life, in a way. It shone between his fingers in the plastic-thin moonlight, it was white. He turned and tried it on the log wall. It drew a thin white stripe after it. Then he drew a large white cross on the door and went in.

But when the next day Tove stood in front of him among the suitcases in the strip of sun in front of the window asking about something, he had no idea what he should answer. He had to think twice to remember what she said, for it was almost as if she hadn't said anything. Not because her voice had changed, but because now he could suddenly hear how self-effacingly, how humbly she had always talked to him, and that up to now he hadn't found anything odd about it. How had it come − − little by little? For there had been a time when her voice sounded entirely different, warm, vibrant, a little husky, a time when he couldn't hear it without having the desire to lift her up and carry her with him, lift this living, trembling voice up to his ear, pour it in through his ear, drink himself drunk with his ear and stagger around with her in his arms until they collapsed together in some dark place. What had become of that voice, what had become of her – – of course she wasn't the same after twelve years, her skin a little duller, her figure by and large the same, but what kind of a dress was that, decent, but of some thick material which didn't suit her, instead of the thin sensitive material she wore when he lifted her up – – suddenly he remembered that he himself had been with her and chosen the thick dress.

What was that she had said – – »Well, how have you managed all this time alone?« There was nothing disturbing about the words, but the fleeting, hunted expression in her eyes, the anxious, eager tone – – she tried to strike the tone she thought he would value, had gradually fallen into a certain routine of choosing the words that called forth his usual torrent about how meaningful and exhausting his work was, his need for peace and consideration – – he sensed she already stood prepared with the next cue, probably: Now you must be careful not to overtax yourself. She was ready for new restrictions, new retreats, could make her voice even more humble, if he needed it – – but it was really just the opposite he needed. What should he say to make her come nearer, lift her own voice up to his ear?

It was more difficult than he had imagined last night. Maybe it was much too precipitate to begin immediately, he had to decide himself, but he couldn't keep on standing here without answering, either. For the present he had to be as he used to be to get over the dead point, and he could easily find the words, they were right on his lips, e.g.: Yes, you can say that again, every time you get to the bottom of something, new depths open up under it, etc., but he noticed he couldn't strike the correct tired-careless tone again. He tried to clear his throat, if only he could clear his throat as he used to do for an opening, the rest would surely come, but his throat was dry and thick, and the sounds it let slip through were hoarse and insignificant, he couldn't accept them as a throat-clearing. In little more than a week he had gotten out of practice in throat-clearing. He bent down and took a suitcase in each hand, heaved them up so abruptly that he could feel the fiber ruptures spread down his back like a run in a stocking.

»Let's get unpacked.«

He woke that night with a strange feeling. It wasn't his heart, not that way, in any case; it beat lively anough, but not nervously, it was more like a surplus of energy. He felt light and free, was capable of anything, he could go right over to her and say what should be said. At first he lay there for a while breathing deeply. It was a long time since he had felt so young and full of life. He was, after all, young and strong, all that about getting old and staid was just imagination, habit − − it was easy, just walk over to her and say: Get up and come with me, it's wonderful outside, there's the scent of rose-hips, don't you smell it, let's take a swim, let's swim out nude, there will be phosphorescence, let's take a golden moonlight swim.

Strange it hadn't occurred to him long ago, he had been sleepwalking for years. He swung his legs quickly out of bed, went over and shook her gently. Kept standing there watching her sleeping childlike face in the faint moonlight, her hair that flowed darkly out over the pillow, the mouth just slightly open so that you caught a glimpse of the white front teeth. He took her hand and patted it gently. She sat up suddenly, and sleep-drugged and frightened stared at him.

128

»What – what is it?« she whimpered. He sat on the edge of the bed and took her hand between his. She looked about, confused, while she alternately held and released his hands, as if she wasn't sure what it was she had gotten ahold of.

»There, there,« he smiled and held her hand tight, »I just wanted to talk with you a little.«

»Yes, yes, but what is . . .«

»I wondered whether we shouldn't take a little walk in the moonlight?«

»Now? But what time is it? I think it's still dark . . .« she squinted at the window and brushed the hair from her eyes.

»It's only four.« He didn't look at his watch, but knew that it must be four. She had wakened a little more and snuggled up against him a moment.

»Ew, I'm cold -- – you frightened me so, I thought . . .«

»Thought what?«

»I can't remember now – – but it would be better to take a walk in the morning, it's so cold now.«

There was no point in talking about swimming now, and especially not nude swimming.

»I just think it's such a wonderful night.«

»Oh, yes, I can see that – – but I think I'd rather wait until tomorrow – – tomorrow early – – does that matter?«

She tucked herself in and closed her eyes.

»No, of course not. Tomorrow early, let's say. It's wonderful to take a walk in the morning, too.«

Villy went over to his bed, cautiously, so as not to lose anything. No, it wouldn't do to go to bed again, then the whole thing would evaporate. He went outside and down toward the beach. Now the sun appeared over the hills by the lighthouse. The gulls flew screeching low over the water. The sand was a little moist and cohesive on top, but loose and light underneath. He was wide awake, it was nearly too much now, he felt the certainty from before ooze out of himself with every prolonged gull cry. The water was fairly rough, it was too light now for nude swimming anyway. He wanted to walk over toward the lighthouse, but the sun hurt his eyes, so he turned around and walked back to the rose-hip thicket again. Precisely. Tomorrow he would lead her through the thicket. They would pick rose-hips, throw them at each other. Who cares about clothes getting a little torn, he wouldn't pay so much attention to that kind of thing any more. A lot of things would be different in the future. He looked at his watch. Almost four-thirty. So the question was, could he keep himself awake -- until seven, for example -- wouldn't he be a little bleary-eyed by then? Wouldn't it really be better to get those few hours' sleep and then be fresh and rested when it counted?

He hurried back to bed, it was so light now that he lay in against the wall on his side so that the light wouldn't get into his eyes, but when he had lain there ten minutes, he hadn't gotten any sleepier. If he lay on his stomach the light wouldn't bother him at all. He lay on his stomach, but the pillow was too soft, he couldn't really catch his breath. He got up on his elbow to fix it. He gave it a quarter turn so that the corners lay up and down and at the sides, but it was still hard to breathe freely even though he put one arm under his head. Then he shook the pillow so that the inmost corner which should lie under his nose got very thin. He bent it in under so his nose reached freely beyond the resulting edge. With his right leg outstretched, his left slightly bent, left arm bent up under his chin and the right down along his side and in under his hip, everything was fine, now he could breathe and wasn't bothered by the light. He shut his eyes and began breathing deeply and regularly, but sleep wouldn't come, he couldn't keep his thoughts away from the titillating areas: tomorrow, in the future . . .

He had to try to relax completely, make himself believe that it wasn't a matter of life and death, it didn't have to be exactly tomorrow. And even though he knew deep inside himself that it was a devious method of enticing sleep, he felt himself getting heavy and relaxed.

When all's said and done, it's just a question of coincidence, he thought before he dropped off completely.

The Pants

Okay, okay, I'll get to the point. I'm in the tiny minority, and so I've got to get to the point. The majority never needs to explain itself, it's explanation enough that they are the majority. Not so many details, you say, but it's not so easy to say off the cuff what's important and what's not. Take the dairyman I trade with, for example, he has a glass eye. So what, you ask; and yet, I recently bought half a pound of butter, and when I went to butter bread for my lunch the lump of butter suddenly gave me a stony stare. Now he has got a larger size of eye, but I was so shocked that I changed to margarine and in that way I got back my childhood taste for margarine on ryebread. So much welled up in me, and I think that made me buy those pants.

You see, as a child I got a bum deal on clothes, I got my brother's old rubber boots, sweaters, lumpy mended socks, coats, books, toys, I made an awful commotion every time, but there were no two ways about it, I had to be a good boy and accept my place in line. But now that I'm alone and getting on in years and can buy my own clothes, I go and rummage in boxes of used clothing, I feel naked in a tailor-made suit. At the second-hand clothing store and at auctions I buy shoes and clothes that have belonged to other people, watches, suspenders, pants, hats, it's a relief to slide into a pair of pants that have been walked in, sat in, and sometimes pissed in, too. A calm comes over me. All my worries fall into the cuffs, ready to pour out every now and then along with the gravel and chaff which usually collects there. Yes, I've noticed that cuffs are out now. Why don't they knock down the street curbs, too, and let the dirt blow around freely? With cuffs you're sure where the dirt is.

With this taste of margarine in my mouth I knew I had to get myself a pair of secondhand pants, I needed to refresh that feeling again. So yesterday I found a pair in a little shop I usually go to. They were dark brown, the seat was beginning to droop, there were a couple of bulges at the knees as if they'd been worn by a horse, but I don't care too much if they fit or look nice. What matters is that they have personality, that they have atmosphere. Of course they had been cleaned after the previous occupant, but I could taste their special scent of something melancholy and faithful, which really appealed to me and at the same time made me excited, I could hardly keep myself from putting them on before I got home. Let me tell you, every time I put on old rags like this, their atmosphere seeps into me and makes me behave differently than I usually do, they draw me towards parts of town where I've never been before, make me talk to total strangers the clothes may know.

These pants drove me down toward the harbor, but not the part I usually go to, they led me out of the main street, the fancy shops disappeared and little bars showed up, but the pants continued on to the last one. You couldn't see what it was like in there, the curtains were drawn, so from the outside it looked really dreary and boring, and who feels like going in there? But I couldn't do a thing, that was the place the pants had decided on.

It wasn't so bad in there, even though there wasn't exactly linen on the tables, there was green linoleum where the dice could really tap dance. Nice people, a little loudmouthed but not really drunk, coats on and caps on the table, so they had to move them every time the dice were about to roll into them, so better on the floor, obviously, there was a terrific back and forth of caps and bottles. I kept my coat on and asked for a beer and a bottle of stout. I was really satisfied with the pants. At first I felt a little uneasy, but now I patted them and enjoyed sitting down without their getting tight around the knees like new ones.

There was a lady sitting by herself in a corner, a pretty woman, in her thirties I would guess, dark coat and fur hat, a sort of Russian style hat, a little full in the face, eyes nearly stout-brown, her mouth looked as if it wanted to cry, but actually I wasn't sitting watching her, I'm finished with that chapter. The last girl I had was named Ruth, and one day as we were lying on the sofa doing it she said just what I needed: your ceiling needs painting, Karl. So it came to a stop all by itself, because it wasn't Ruth or anyone else I was interested in, it was a small frightened girl long ago, it had something to do with wet trees and benches, little hands in big pockets and big hands in little ones and a treat of rum balls and chocolate mints, that was what I couldn't forget, everything else was just cotton and bandages. Of course I kicked Ruth out, but I ought to be damned grateful to her for that line, it could not have been said more plainly. After that time I began to buy my beer at different places, my consumption increased, you know, and I don't like to be conspicuous. Stout and schnapps, alcohol to clean the greasy thoughts with. Okay, I'll get to the point, but all of this is part of what happened. You should damned well be more nervous that I'm forgetting something, because *I* am. Let me see now, about that lady, it was something with the pants, either they caught sight of her or she caught sight of them. She looked over at me, but I think she looked at the pants, too, and then she lifted her glass, put it down again, looked around for the waiter but then looked over at me again, or at the pants, when he caught her glance. I can only see one explanation for her nervousness: there was something between her and those pants, maybe she had been expecting the pants but not with me in them. And then a remarkable thing – – here you must promise not to interrupt me – – the pants began to get tight around the knees, they made me stand up and walk over to her. Yes, maybe you don't see anything strange in that, you think to yourself: what an old tom cat. But that's because you haven't paid attention to the details, they're what's important. The pants wanted to go over to her, and for reasons of modesty I had to go along. So there I sat. And the pants couldn't talk, I had to speak up for them, and at first I sat there and tried to figure out what they wanted.

Well, of course at first I said, what would you like to drink? Idiotic: she was sitting there with a glass of liqueur.

»Thanks, I have one,« she said. Look, it's here I think we have a clue. Otherwise she might have said: will you leave me alone, just what do you take me for? Or this: thanks, honey, what can you afford? But she said what I said, and I think that must be proof she knew those pants pretty well. As soon as I had sat down, she put her hands up on the table and rested them there. I thought: now we've got to figure this out, take it easy – – if those pants want something it will be clear. And so I sat as quiet as a mouse and felt it penetrate me. Something was wrong somewhere. Someone had been hurt, maybe her, or him in the pants, or both of them. A clamminess came from the pants that sent goose pimples up my thighs.

I stared at her hands lying right across from mine. Her fingertips lightly touched the green tabletop. My own carrots were lying in the same way, and my square, yellow, cracked fingernails stared right at hers, which were elegant, translucent like the petals of a flower you hold up to the light. Then she turned her fingers in under her palms, and at that my fingers really went crazy, they reached across toward hers, crept over the table and reached under hers in order to open them again, but it was still the pants that were behind all this, and she didn't move her hands, she didn't open them either, but let my fingers stay there half-way under hers, and it was only then I looked. Her eyes were round and black now, I thought at first it was me she was looking at, but it was something behind me.

»What's going on here?« a shrill, jagged voice like a boy's who is trying to make his voice sound grownup, so I was a little flabbergasted to see a gigantic man step up to the table. I drew my fists back. Her hands jumped into her purse and hid.

»Not a thing, it was just . . .« She tried to smile, I guess she wanted to say: it was just the pants, but that wouldn't have been understood in the right spirit. I kept my trap shut, I didn't get any orders from the pants.

I disliked his face instantly, but that, too, has to be under-stood in the right spirit, because I have friends who look at least just as unpleasant without it bothering me, the same small, distrustful foxy eyes in a big puffy mug, the same broad, self-righteous mouth, I've never been able to under-stand what pleasure women can get from a face like that, but they were good buddies, and I think he and I could have had many good drinks together, too, if we had met each other and I hadn't those pants on.

»Did he bother you?«

»No, not at all, we were having a chat, it's nothing at all.«

A chat. We'd hardly said a word. Honestly, I was moved by the way she covered for me, even though it was the pants she was worried about, but at the same time she said it was nothing at all. I was moved and relieved and at the same time damned mad at the way women humiliate themselves for men and are afraid of them because they are big, self-confident and jealous. I got up. He moved in front of me.

»Do you have to go now, just when I've arrived, that's kind of strange,« he said sweetly.

It helped a little to stand up, even if he was still a head taller than me. But in the course of time I've learned that the worst thing you can do when you're next to tall people is to lay your head back and address their nostrils, they really enjoy that and hold their noses just so, inhale blissfully and clap you on the shoulder as if they were forgiving you some old debt. I stared right at the knot of his tie, which was very full and neat as opposed to mine, which looks like a tied-off intestine, and said:

»Yes, now that you mention it, it is rather strange. I'll go and think it over a little.«

Then he stepped aside. The crap shooters had become quiet, I heard only her trying to straighten things out.

»I'm telling you, he was so polite . . .«

»Yes, anyway he shook your hand, I saw.«

I waded out into the cold. It was windy, the pants flapped around me. I hurried away from the place.

Now fall had come. When I had tramped out there I didn't give it much thought, I was more anxious to know where we were going, me and the pants. But now I saw it. Haven't you ever noticed that it can be fall for a long time before you actually realize it. Of course, you know it, for sure, and if someone asked: what season is it now? you would answer right away: fall, of course. But suddenly one day you see it, the leaves lying trampled on the wet flagstones, the wind up the pantlegs, you feel some strange sinking motions in your heart, ugh, it's fall now, and you are surprised that it first strikes you now, even though you've been aware of it for several weeks, but in such an absent-minded way, but now you're caught up in it yourself and can't get out of it just like that even if you wanted to. You are yourself one of the greasy leaves being trampled awry, there isn't a damned thing you can do about it. By the way, it's something the same with spring now that I think about it – – ok, ok, fine, we'll stick to fall. As I said I was walking along staring at the fallen leaves, I must have been really feeling low because I don't remember anything but cobblestones and paving, cigarette butts, dog turds, tin foil, there was an incredible amount of tin foil, the kind that candy bars, chocolate mints and that sort of thing are wrapped in, that's about the saddest thing you can see, that kind of discarded, crumpled tin foil that's been walked on by wet shoes. I was walking along there and was really unhappy about that story, but I thought to myself, it won't do a damned bit of good, you should just keep out of it, those two will figure it out, forget it, it's not like you to take it so hard, think of your own troubles, maybe that will cheer you up a little. And that's what I did, yes, indeed it was easy enough, all too easy, I went and slipped on the dead tin foil. She was really afraid of me, the kid was. I didn't want to hurt her, but the only thing that would calm her down was chocolate mints, I stuffed her with chocolate mints, but there weren't enough chocolate mints in the country to quiet her down, the poor kid. Seventeen, I think she was, and I was in my early twenties. I had had several, but never in that way, there was none of that sort of thing, I wanted to make her happy, she was like a little sister, I've only had brothers, a sister to take good care of, give some nice clothes to, be kind and polite to, take along to some of the good movies, get to smile now and then – – now don't interrupt me, or else I'd rather just shut up.

Well, it didn't work out. And the worst of it is that I saw her later. It was enough to drive you to drink, if you didn't already. I myself had gone out looking for a pickup, on my way into one of those places with red neon lights over the door and a people-wise, unfriendly doorkeeper right inside the door, and I step aside for a couple coming out, a fat guy with a girl, it was her, thank God she didn't see me. She was laughing loudly about something or other, but I could have done without that laughter. It wasn't a matter of chocolate mints anymore, it wasn't a matter of anything. There simply aren't enough chocolate mints in the world.

Yes, so there I was walking along brooding with my hands in my pockets and my chin between my lapels. I didn't see where I was going until I suddenly stopped at the edge of the pier. There was a strong wind, the water sprayed up toward me. It was cold to stand so far out, but still I stayed there, I don't know, the whole thing was strange. Your ceiling needs painting. And what then, once it's been painted?

Actually I had gotten pretty far out along the pier. Nobody lived here, just locked warehouses and naked cranes the wind was whistling through. A single, unlighted coal barge lay creaking in its moorings, otherwise all the boats were snug and secure farther inside the harbor, and there were lights and people and bars in there too. By now the two of them had gotten home and they were fighting about me, or about him who was the first to wear the pants. Maybe he beat her up, he actually looked the type, the big bully, because he didn't get ahold of me. And she probably bawled and cringed, warded him off with her fur hat and purse. But at the same time maybe she thought she deserved it because of what she had done to the other guy, hurt him so he left and stayed away for several days. That had surely happened over and over and he had returned every time, but women want to see how far they can go, it's as if they want to figure out something that way, how pretty they are, how impossible to do without. But in the end she figured it wrong after all, went a bit too far, and then he came out here just like me, and then, I guess, he jumped into the drink.

But that was all that stuff I didn't want to think about anymore, and I didn't want to rack my brain about my own fate, either, how was I going to entertain myself then, think ahead − − of new margarine sandwiches, of new drinking buddies who are so well supplied with their own miseries that you don't feel like mentioning your own − − there also might be something at the movies worth seeing, but I've stopped that too. I can't concentrate anymore on what goes on on the screen. What's happening is down in the theater. There are so many people around me who have each other to sit by, a big hand and a small hand meet in a bag of licorice drops so it rips and the drops spill down under the seats like dice, the chocolate mints are broken in half and like a gentleman he gives her all the tin foil − − no, I don't get much out of the movie and way too much out to the rest, so I'd rather have some colored bottles at home, sit and stare at the ceiling. It needs to be painted. Ant what happens when it's painted. And why were you afraid of me, you poor little thing, I just wanted the best for you. Oh, Jesus Christ, one should stop thinking for good.

There was a sort of landing place right down at the water's edge, like a drawer that's pulled out. I walked down the stone steps and tried to stop thinking. The water was sloshing up. I shuffled back and forth and was about to go up again but suddenly one of my shoes took a good gulp, it really went in, what the hell, it had been a while since I'd washed my feet, so I stood still and let the water splash around my shoelaces. Just stop trying to figure things out. After all, you have stopped so much, why not stop that too, why not stop completely − − be free, get off − − cross your heart, is there anyone who would miss you? I stood and froze with my hands in my pockets, my lighter was in there, out with it. There wasn't even a splash, at least not one that differed from the other splashes and noises. One splash among the others. Just a foretaste. My pipe was in the left pocket, out with it, now you've stopped smoking at the same time. Then off with your coat. It lay on top of the water for a while and tried to calm the waves a little with sleeves spread out, to comfort them a bit. One of the tails sank, still it stayed afloat, there was probably a little air left in the pockets. That irritated me. My shoes were wet anyway. I couldn't get the laces untied, so I tore them loose. One went too far out, the other one landed in the middle of the coat, then it finally began to sink. Now I was really freezing, but that didn't matter, that was also one of the things I wanted to stop doing. I sunk at the knees and stretched out my arms, but that was too much like the starting position at swimming meets, and in this case it was a matter of not swimming. It was probably better to just step over the edge and let oneself sink. Then it occurred to me that I've always hated getting water in my ears. I rooted around in my jacket pockets, there was everything else there but cotton. However, my tobacco was in the inside pocket, so I stuck a good plug into each ear. Now I should be ready. But which leg should go first? I tried to remember which leg I usually start with, but that's one of those things you never seriously try to get firmly established, and then when it really counts, you're left standing there. In that situation you simply lack know-how. I could also take off sideways, or backwards, or I could lie down and roll off the edge. The longer I remained standing, the more confused I got because of the many possibilities. The pantlegs by now were sopping wet at the bottom and were plastered around my shins, the pants really ought to be able to give me a clue, it was they that had started all this. I stared down at them, and then my knees began to shake, but now it wasn't because of the cold. It was the pants that wanted to come down here, it was them who wanted me to do kneebends at the water's edge, because it's dead certain that I've never claimed that existence was magnificent, on the contrary, life is troublesome, but still it has certain advantages, such as stout, nope it was those damned pants that had the terrible itch to get down to the drowned candidate. He might have had a pair of new, blameless pants on that day and left the old ones in the lurch, and now they wanted to go down to him, but that had to be without me. Quick as a flash I got them off and threw them out. First one leg sank and fluttered back and forth under the water as if it was looking for something, then the other one joined it, and then they agreed completely, that was exactly the direction they had to go, and in half a second they pulled the sagging bottom and everything with them. I raised the jacket collar up around my ears, hurried up the steps and homeward.

I understand very well that you did a doubletake when you saw me at full gallop heading down the street in my jacket, underwear and wet socks, but this is the pure, absolute truth, and the reason I didn't stop the first time you shouted was probably because of the tobacco in my ears, I almost couldn't get it out again. And I don't mind, either, staying overnight here at the station tonight, chief, I realize it won't do any good to claim that I am more sober than I've been for a long time — — and if to top it off you would loan me a pair of pants to wear home tomorrow morning. But you've got to promise me one thing: I'd like to know a little about the pants first, whether they belonged to a rummy, a pimp, or maybe a male prostitute. You can certainly understand that I've become more particular after this experience.

142

The Passage

As much as possible I don't go out during the day. The numerous people, the blinding light, the ceaseless noise make my nerves bristle, my thoughts boil over, taking my strength from me, I suddenly get the idea that I can't get wet, I can never get wet again, water will bounce off me as if I were coated with a film, plastic or something like that, the sun shines, not a cloud in the sky, let alone a raindrop, I walk by a lake, should I throw myself in, I have to have it proven, the sooner the better, just a decision, but I'm shy with other people, no, I have to make the attempt in private, on the sly, behind closed doors, and I increase my pace, maybe I'm on my way some place, but that must wait, I have to call tonight and say I've gotten sick on the way, this is more urgent, maybe I really am sick, for it must be a kind of sickness if I can't get wet, a really unfortunate sickness at that for I've never heard of it, so it's highly likely they haven't found any remedy or serum for it, I become more and more uneasy, begin to trot, I'd rather not attract attention, but if you only trot a little, it will look as if you're busy like all the others, and I am busy, I almost can't wait, I force myself to rush up them in long leaps, my knees sink from the exertion when I stand on top, but there isn't time to catch my breath, I've already gotten the key out, want to come in, out to the kitchen, turn on the faucet, I thrust my arm under the cold jet, jacket and all, and feel the water, it's there, I can nearly taste it with my skin, delicious cold water, it streams inside my shirt down under my elbow and collects there, it's nearly too good to be true, but I have to try the other arm, too, I tear off my shoes and socks, toes up in the sink, yes, they get wet, really wet, but my body, then, I tear my shirt aside, fill the hollow of my hand with water and splash it against my stomach, gasping, notice that I get wet, it seeps down into my underpants, down my thighs, I get goosebumps, I get tears in my eyes, in some miraculous way I've been saved at the last moment, who knows what would have happened if I'd arrived two minutes later, I promise myself to stay home the rest of the day.

But along toward evening I cant't endure sitting at home any longer. Loneliness, the yellow glare from the lightbulb and the silence which seems to expect something of me make me nauseous. Then I go down to the passage. Maybe I'm just plain going downhill, but I've lived so many years now in my room's level plane, slept on my bed's level plane, been fiddling with left-over numbers in the level plane of my office. That's certainly enough.

The passage itself isn't any downhill path. A really nice passage between two large streets having one-way traffic each in its own direction. During the day a shortcut, a sluice where the water level between the two traffic arteries is equalized, delayed busy people cut through the passage with sharp briefcases, at particular allotted times they are the ones who characterize the passage, the busy stream from one side collides with and splits up the delayed wave from the other, briefcases intertwine, shoot up to the surface and cut it for a way like shark fins, hostile eddies rise, but the pressure of business and obligations easily win out over aggression and fury, the shark bite is postponed until people take their places in offices.

I sit in my room trying to take stock of my memory. It's evening, but I try to keep the passage out of my thoughts, it's the past that matters now; if it's strong and vivid enough, if one can really document to himself that he has lived, then to that extent the present can't lead you up the garden path. I entice myself with a beer. When you've drunk half of it, you'll have remembered so and so much, and before you've sunk the last of it you should be finished with the day's assignment and it's there, too, summers on Fyn, winters in Norway, my childhood's brook with tadpoles and pike which stood out as sharp and round as I could wish in the dim light of the room, but the more I dig out, the more I distrust my memory, it must be a lie, it must be a question of delusion, it can't be that that's constituted my life, something must lie behind or in among it which I can't grasp, something that can show me why my life has become like this, why I've ended up in the passage, so I can discover the mistake and start over again. All the rest, that which I happily remember, must be an act, a performance, meant to keep me outside as a spectator, I can clap or criticize, but the play is finished, it's been completed without my being able to do anything about it.

The passage, a place you pass in haste, but a place where you also linger. Along toward evening it's as though all the haste and bustle have deposited something else along its banks, people have remained standing, walk around among each other, shuffle back and forth, look in shop windows, glance at the others who've stopped in their vicinity. Two-thirds of the passage is roofed with colonnades, but in the middle there's a square opening. When the stars are coming out there's just room for three or four constellations and the fringes of others. A single bright star to the right of a gable no doubt belongs to Orion, but I've never gotten it corroborated. I'll have to go out of the passage, out on the street to figure it out, but I continually postpone it, promise myself to take a proper look when I go home, when I leave the passage late in the evening, I usually have so much else in my head and in my pockets that I forget it.

The starlit flagstones under the square aren't used much

long it would be remarkable if one of them didn't say some-thing now. She's already scraping her heels a little, not exactly impatiently, but, still, and he's cleared his throat a couple of times. But I still keep my distance so as not to thwart the great moment. The eternal stream of water splashes in the basin, the stars lean forward, peeking down from the gallery, the footsteps in the other arcade stop, I hold my breath, and finally he says: Unusually beautiful, the tiles . . . It's said into the air, could, for that matter, have been aimed at me, but it was for just that reason I stood a little to the side so that she was closest. She doesn't have to pick up the thread and for just that reason she can make a little nose-sound – – hn – – which could mean anything at all, so she both stands there as a nice girl and at the same time has given the green light. Then the time has come. I enter from the right, move close to him, now I can no longer distract him, he's already forming the next, the decisive sentence, and now he turns away from the tiles and glances at her, I'm a little worried for his sake, don't you think you should have waited just a bit with that, pal, I think, but good luck anyway, and then he says: But of course that's just my opinion, tastes differ after all . . . The nose-sound isn't enough any more. She has either to toss her head and leave or remain standing there and make up her mind about his taste, and to my great joy I hear her say – – while, for appearance's sake, she steps a centimeter away from him: Yes, in a way . . . But even before she'd said it my hand had been down in his jacket pocket and come up again with a little box and very gently conveyed the loot into my own pocket without the wrapping rustling the least little bit. They exchange a few more remarks, but I don't hear them, I'm satisfied now and leave them to themselves. Even while the two finally take their eyes from the Finnish tiles and turn toward the fountain and for the first time will make a mutual decision, namely whether they should walk on the inside or out around the splashing basin which is filled and filled yet never runs over, I'm on my way out of the passage with my plunder which I now squeeze and rustle recklessly between my fingers down in my pocket, so desirous of getting the box home to the rest of my treasure that as usual I completely forget to check out the rest of the constellation Orion.

When I get home, I torment myself a little, first go out and put on the water for tea, take my shoes off without damaging the laces, step into my slippers, being careful not to tread down the back, force myself to observe all the little time-consuming considerations I normally don't care about in order to draw out the pleasure, take away the plates with the remains of the dinner, rinse them off under the warm water faucet, a bit of gravy won't let go, I hold the plate at different angles, but only when I hold it nearly on end is the tough brown crust peeled away. Then I can't hold out any longer, I rush out into the entryway to my coat and tear open the box, yes, sure enough, a box of Smith Brothers, but I'm completely exhausted from the endured exicitement and have to lean against the doorframe a moment. Then I go into the living room and sit down heavily in a chair, pick up a cough drop, hold it up to the light, let the raised patterns play a moment in the lamplight, then guide it in between my lips, let it slide between my teeth and upper lip from one side to the other, then down in my lower lip, after that under my tongue from where it's difficult to get out again, it's now become thinner and smoother, infinitely slowly I let it dissolve, and even while I draw out its enjoyment to a silk thin, movable taste spot, which immediately fastens itself to a place where it can no longer be dis-

ment looking down into the basin, puts out her hand to stroke the boy on the head but gives it up and continues on across the flagstones. He follows guietly.

Sometimes I'm obsessed by the feeling that what I'll find in the pocket is neither a comb nor a change purse nor dice, but a hand, a real living hand. It doesn't frighten me, Oh, yes, I get palpitations at the thought, but that doesn't keep me from sneaking my hand down, on the contrary, maybe that's the best thing that could happen, a warm living hand grabbing hold of mine – – hard and angry it would surely be, but anyway that'd be far better than all the cigarette lighters and pipe cleaners, at one fell swoop I'd handle the problem of having to piece an existence together from all these things some of which I have far too many specimens of, cigarette lighters e.g., while I need a bunch more of other things and need to play my tricks for many years yet, reaping numerous trivial lighters and scooter keys before I have what I must have. I have eighteen nail cleaners, but only one pair of scissors, I got up to twenty combs before I got a fine-toothed one. Twenty-three ball point pens, but still no pencil, isn't that strange? How many ball point pens are there to a pencil. Just a stub, I'm willing to sharpen it myself. How many screwdrivers are there to an adjustable wrench? How many Anacin to one penicillin? I can see it's a nearly impossible task to carry out considering I'm thirty-four, sooner or later I will have to say stop and then begin with what I have, try to get the best out of it, but in the meantime I keep up my courage, anyway, it would be risky business to throw yourself out into a new existence without something as elementary as a pencil. But maybe a hand would be just the thing to make me dare the leap.

I remained standing there watching them as they walked out of the passage, he two steps behind her all the while. I tried to feel what it was I'd got hold of, a somewhat triangular metal object, probably yet another cigarette lighter, but of a shape I couldn't recognize. I left the passage at the other end. For once I remembered to look up at Orion, but it turned out that this constellation couldn't be seen from this side, but only from where the two had left.

I let go of the object in my pocket and walked calmly home. A cigarette lighter could no longer excite me now. When I'd gotten home and had made tea, I picked it up to put it in the drawer with the rest of the cigarette lighters. When I have to some day, I'll select a few of them and part with the rest. But I remained standing there with it in my hand in front of the drawer. Then I went back to the desk where there was more light. It was a revolver. It was quite small, the barrel was short, and the metal guard protecting the trigger was shaped so that the object felt triangular, and thus my error. But what should I do with it? I needed things with which to construct my life, but not an object to destroy life, neither others' nor my own. I had to get rid of it. Perhaps right now he stood with her on a dark staircase or on a quay, stood fishing in his pocket for it, and it wasn't there. I was on the way out the door, but stopped on the stairs. The light went off. So I went back in and put it in a drawer which only held an arch support, which I then put into the drawer with the hernia belts. I didn't have to carry it, I didn't have to use it, it could just lie there for years. But someday a situation could arise which might go differently if it hadn't been there. Now I knew it was there, and that it was loaded. I thought for a moment about firing it, emptying it at the constellation Orion, but it was too late, I should have done it right away. It was already a part of my life, and I laid it back in the drawer.

Sometimes I can't remember my name. At the office people seldom use my name, when someone does refer to

rum, and anyway we used juice at home – – but there is a little black current rum, at worthy compromise, a proper slug on it.

I serve the sago soup with black current rum to myself and my glove guest on the glass table. I eat a few spoonfuls, it tastes heavenly and warms me right down to my navel. Then I pick up the glove, fill it with the sliding spoonfuls like the clumps of frogs eggs I found in the brook as a child. As long as I hold it up, the fingers bristle like cow teats, but now I set it down on the glass table, close the opening tightly with my left hand and smooth and shape it with my right. It's a little too full, it now turns out, I unload a little onto my plate, and now I bring out the glove's natural shape and smoothness, it lies there with real plump fingers like the hand of a black princess. It steams a little with an inner glow, I bend over to press a kiss against it when I catch sight of the blood. It gives me a start, a dark pool of blood spreads out under the hand. But I immediately realize that it's the thin part of the sago soup that's slowly leaking out. I lift the glove sadly and see how sticky it is underneath, I lick the good rum juice off, it tastes good, I squeeze the glove a little so more comes out, I press the hand so a whole small stream comes out of a finger, I stick the fingers in my mouth one by one and suck on them, I lean back and suck on them, chew, bite softly my sago-udder. I'm happy right now, but can I be satisfied with this for long? – – And at the same time I think: in the future I won't dream of having sago soup any other way.

This Past Year

Now I don't know how much you have figured out without my help, so some of what I'm telling you, you probably know already. You probably know, too, that a year ago I was in Fyn for a few days to bury my mother. I didn't return home unexpectedly, my wife knew very well I'd be coming home that Thursday around eight o'clock in the evening. Even by the time I got to the second floor I heard the commotion, glass being smashed, wood being splintered – – strange that none of the neighbors had intervened, maybe they weren't home. I go all the way up and let myself in, hang up my coat, put down my suitcase and open the door to the living room. Everything is smashed, fragments of glass, chair legs, books everywhere, paintings broken in two, the table overturned, and the lamps – – but the windows were unbroken I remember, that was really remarkable. And the two of them were apparently unhurt. They didn't have a stitch of clothing on, stood a few meters from each other, my wife with a vase in her hand, the last unbroken one, he with a large black revolver pointed right at her stomach. I didn't know the man, couldn't remember having seen him there anyway. There wasn't anything particularly characteristic about him. If he'd had clothes on, maybe I could have recognized him. His penis hung down, but was a little swollen and reddish – – that, along with their nakedness, told me there had been something between them recently. But after that things had obviously run afoul.

My wife was very white except for her cheeks, they were

lowered, she was naturally quiet and didn't have much to do with anyone.

Eventually, coming with all the papers at once wasn't enough, I divided them into smaller piles so I had more occasions to go in to her. I became happier about my work and ate well.

Then a time came when I found myself somewhat ridiculous, I collected the invoices throughout the day and came in with them just a little before closing time. I wasn't eating much, often felt nauseous. That went on for a couple of weeks until one evening I came into the office a little too late, she had just gone, had laid a black plastic cover over the adding machine. Next morning I went in to her immediately and asked whether she had seen the pile I had left for her the day before? It was a fairly large pile. Yes, she'd gotten them and they were all recorded.

»Well, but don't you think we should get married, then?« She didn't really know.

Six months later we agreed to get married. We didn't talk much together, we left it to each other to make decisions, we almost took turns deciding things. There was never a bad word between us. I still don't understand what has happened, and I didn't understand it then a year ago, either, so it wasn't easy to go into it. Sometimes I could forget it completely, things were nearly the same as in the old days, and I figured that she, too, had erased it from her mind.

Our sex life wasn't completely satisfying, she often seemed a little distracted when I came into her room, but then I'd let her alone, just pat her hair a little and tell her she should try to get some sleep. I figured it would surely be my turn again someday. Besides that, we lived as usual and the children were good and didn't notice anything.

Oh, yes, now I remember one time there seemed to be something brewing. One evening I'd been down to the street to buy some cheroots in the automat, and when I got back up she quickly tried to hide a bottle under the table, and the glass she'd just poured tipped over into her skirt.

»Well, are you drinking on the sly?« It was said kindly and a bit jokingly to her.

»Yes, I take a little one now and then.« She sounded breathless.

»Well,« I said, »that's all right, but you can feel free to drink while I'm here.«

»Oh, can I?« she said. And then up with the bottle again, she pours a glass and gives it to me.

»No, thanks,« I said, »I just get sleepy from it, drink it yourself.«

Then she swills it down, something red, Dubonnet or something like that.

»You consider yourself too good to drink with me, don't you?« she said and then her cheeks got red. »You feel you're better than me, you despise me, you think I'm a bad wife, a bad mother, just say it,« she shouted.

I tried to reassure her, but she poured a fresh glass.

»It's your share I'm drinking now,« she said and down it went. Then she dropped the glass, but it didn't break, just rolled around on the carpet. Shortly after, she was suddenly on her knees in front of me, crying with her head on my pants. I got her to her feet and in to bed. But I mustn't leave, she wanted me right up against her, and I lay down with her. Just as soon as I entered her, she laid her head back, all the way out over the edge of the bed and looked as though she had lost consciousness. I got scared and pulled out again, but she grabbed hold of me and shouted: Keep going, man! And I stuck it in again, and she laid her head back, turned up the whites of her eyes and then I didn't hear any more from her.

The next day she was calm and quiet once more, and it continued that way for a year's time. I always had the revolver in my inside pocket, I was nervous about putting it down where she could find it.

A week before it happened she boozed quite a bit, no longer on the sly, and two days previously she sent the children out to her parents. I could see that she was at a difficult point, so I let her alone. Maybe she had talked to him again, I didn't ask her about anything. I thought, it has to take its time. At that point we hadn't had any sex life for a month, so we each slept in our own rooms. She didn't call me, and I controlled myself.

That night, she came into my room and turned on the light. It must have been four o'clock. I sat up blinking my eyes and discovered that she was stark naked. Maybe she'd drunk a bit, too, her hair was a little tousled and her cheeks were flushed. I thought at first she wanted to come in with me and I moved over against the wall, but she said in a very loud voice: Get up and take off your clothes.

I wasn't completely awake yet, but could see then that she was beside herself, so I got up and took off my pajamas. I stood there freezing. She looked at me for a moment. Aha! she said then. Suddenly she sprang over to the closet and began to tear my clothes from the hangers and rummage through the pockets. I got the feeling it was the revolver she was after and went over to her. Quite so, she had gotten it dug out from the pile of clothes just as I brought her tumbling down. I fell into the closet too, we lay there rummaging around on the floor, wrapping ourselves in each other's arms and legs, but I got hold of the revolver and didn't let go. I got out of the closet first and stood up, she crawled out shortly after, removed the ties and shirts that had wrapped themselves around her and stood up in front of me. I nearly couldn't recognize her. Her face was so distorted and wrinkled that she looked older than her own mother.

»So out with it,« she said very quietly, »bawl me out, shoot, let me have it, demand an explanation. Shouldn't I repent? Shouldn't I account for myself? Well, out with it!«

I said it was best if we talked it over the next day – – we were both a little tired, I said, and I had to go to work in the morning.

»Tomorrow. You certainly don't think there's going to be any tomorrow – – there won't be any tomorrow, don't you realize that?«

I began to get afraid. Asked what she meant by that?

»You couldn't care less about me,« she said and came toward me. I pulled back so she wouldn't get hold of the revolver.

»That's just nonsense.«

»Why haven't you questioned me? Why haven't you chased me off or beaten me?«

»Why should I do that?« All the while I stumbled backward from her and had to watch out not to fall over shoes and other things lying around on the floor, still, I got my foot caught in a pair of suspenders that hung out from the bottom of the closet, and was about to fall as I tried to shake them off – – when quick as lightning she grabbed hold of the suspenders and pulled – – luckily they popped off my foot with a snap so we both fell on our backsides, she over by the window, I against the door, which didn't open, however. It turned out later that she had locked it.

We kept sitting there a while, puffing. I made sure that the revolver wasn't pointing at her so as not to provoke her. I wanted to say that it was a misunderstanding, that I just wanted to be good to her and avoid irritating her, but as I sat there I began to sweat, on my forehead, on my upper lip, in my hands, under my arms, between my legs, I shook and sweated, I said:

»Who was he? What did you want with him?«

She didn't answer but sat up against the wall and began to stroke herself up and down her legs.

»Have you seen him since?«

She slowly pulled her hair out into two long wisps which she laid crisscross in front of her mouth and kissed.

»Why was he standing there pointing at you with the revolver? What had you said to each other? You knew I was coming home, why weren't you more careful? Was it to provoke me?«

She held her breasts, let them hop a little in her hands, pushed them together so the nipples met as if crosseyed.

»Why did he stand there pointing at you with a revolver? Why?«

It had become heavy in my hand, I could just barely hold it up, my hands were sweating, too, but I didn't dare put it down.

She began to pull on her nipples, first one, then the other, they got long and elastic, and my penis began to stir, too. I put the revolver in my lap and tried to find a more or less dry spot on my body where I could wipe my sticky hands.

»What do you want with the revolver?« I asked.

She spread her thighs and stuck two fingers into herself.

»Say something else,« she said and lay her head backward, »I can do it best when you talk to me.«

I crawled on all fours over to her and said things I've never thought and never meant.

164

»You whore. You trash bucket. Frigid slut. Prick automat. Bitch.«

And along that vein.

Sweat ran into my eyes and blinded me so I couldn't get my hand out when she threw herself on me. We rolled around on the floor, I held tightly onto the revolver, but she grabbed hold with both hands, with her toes, with her knees, with her thighs.

»Bitch, bitch,« I gasped.

Then a strange, weak pop sounded, not a bang but a muffled boom as if it were packed in wool and rags. She loosened her grip and laid herself back on the floor, turned up the whites of her eyes. I released her and got to my feet, discovered the blood that poured out from between her legs. The revolver lay there in her lap and blood. My hands were bloody, and my stomach and knees, but it wasn't me who'd been hit. I don't know which of us pulled the trigger. I don't know whether she knew, either.

I've always been a little slow on the uptake, and now, after thirty-eight years, have figured out that it's better if you talk together about things while there's time. That's why I've let them summon you now, after having refused to speak for many months, I know very well it's a few mail calls too late, and I don't know if I have much of anything to look forward to now, but life expectancy has increased a good deal in my time, so I imagine I'll get something out of it.

First I picked up the phone and called an ambulance. Then I broke the door and went out and washed and got dressed.

You're my court-appointed lawyer, but you won't have to defend me, though, I'll plead guilty. And compos mentis. Maybe I should be placed under psychiatric observation for a while because I can't sleep at night. She comes and touches me and is loving towards me, but I can't move, I just lie there asking: »Who was he? What did you want with the revolver?« and things like that. It's probably best if I go into a place where I can talk to someone.

The Pillows

It will be a big day tomorrow, and a difficult day, what demand will be made, what bill presented, which leg will you
be kicked on, which shoulder patted? Impossible to say,
dream sweetly, but one day is seldom like another, some
day you're in a completely different place, look down yourself, have gotten a heap of unintentional flesh on your
bones, have experienced and forgotten a series of events,
it's crazy, man, you have awakened in a wrong place, are
the wrong number that's come up, you hurry back to sleep
and hope that these surroundings, this flesh, these memories will shrink to natural size so you can wake up with a
real yawn in a familiar place and fling your normal body
weight without stomach, rolls of fat, or corns out into the
everyday, you lay your ear on the pillow to shut out these
strange voices, and at once one side of you remembers that
it was precisely with pillows themselves it began, quite ordinary pillows: dark, slightly dusty velvet pillows with trim-
mings and ostrich patterned embroidery, round oblong
cushions with fringes and tassels and the aroma of cigars,
flat red sitting cushions with coarse woven topsides, pale
and smooth and naked in the belly, I took care of them all
in turn. Started school too soon, always the smallest, tried
to make myself even smaller, hide behind trees in the
schoolyard, behind bicycle racks, behind a book, behind a
soda, was found anyway and hauled out by those who were
a little bigger, really with no hope of seeing an end to it
back then. As hot-tempered, as full of spit and vinegar as I
was, I refused tooth and nail to fight with anyone bigger

than I was, so I was frequently yanked out like a worm and massacred.

Someday I'll tell my kids the whole story in a language they can understand. Tomorrow will be a big day for them, too, not easy to get through, but, my God, they haven't had an easy time of it lately, nor have I with all the splinters in my hands and dust in my nose.

These familiar pillows I stacked one above the other and gave them names of tormentors: Kaj twerp, Eigil wretch, Søren shit. Always several at once, I screamed with drawn coat hanger or stick: Come on, cowards, many against one, I'm not afraid of you! Pillows in front, to the rear, to the side, surrounded by pillows, I had to be quick as lightning, and over my back all the time so as not to be taken by surprise, but sooner or later I succeeded in getting the decisive thrust in, deep into one of them, I jabbed, angry and ripping and then slaughtered away so the feathers gushed out. At the sight of that the others surrendered immediately. I flung them into their places and swept up the blood and entrails.

»It's strange how thin and floppy the pillows have become,« grunted my father.

»Yes, and several of them are torn – – I sew and sew, but they don't last,« complained my mother.

»Can it be the kid has something to do with it?«

My mother passed the question along to me.

»I just play with them.«

»Yes, but how do you play with them, are you rough with them?«

»Only if they're nasty.«

»Are they?«

»Pretty much.«

Mother bought new pillows, embroidered new cases and handed the old ones over to me. It was well done, my parents were good parents, on the whole I was satisfied with them.

So I had all the old pillows interned in with me, they stood in the corner, waiting to be done for, stacked up on each other, but at night took advantage of the dark and my defenselessness to sneak up on me. I woke up with a scream, turned on the light and tried to look at all of them at once, my eyes screwed up, to see whether any of them had moved. Got up and tied the most sinister one firmly to a chair or a table leg. Fell asleep again with my stick on top of the quilt. The next morning the presumptuous ones got a well-deserved smacking before I went to school.

Gradually the school wallopings ebbed out, I was a friendly type who willingly let others cut ahead in line, but other enemies arose, teachers, my parents at times. The pillows didn't fall into disuse until I became an apprentice.

It was in a grocery. The boss was a rather irritable character, the clerk forced me to buy perverse magazines for him and frequently forgot to reimburse me for them. Then I went over to the stockroom and walloped away on the sacks of peas, prunes, or sugar. Sometimes I thrust my hand down through the stitching on top instead — when you coaxed it long enough you could finally get your hand pushed through and sneak up a slim handful of almonds or brown sugar — it couldn't be noticed in a hundred pound sack.

As a soldier it was bayonet practice that caught my greatest interest. When you rushed at the helpless suspended sacks, jabbed the bayonet in and twisted it around and flayed the stomach canvas open with a tug so kapok poured out, it brought relief and redress for numerous ballings out and punitive marches from the sergeant. Both he and the lieutenant and the old timers teased me because I wasn't so hard-boiled, I hissed their numbers or names between my teeth before I slit them open, 56, 108, Swine, rrritsch! In this way I got along well with my soldier-buddies by and large. All that lies before death, as maybe does everything I'm telling, I'm not completely sure, maybe I'm dead now, but as a party in the case I'm not the right one to make a statement, maybe I'll be irrevocably dead tomorrow, in any case it will be a difficult day, but I may be allowed the hope I'll get the chance to tell my kids these things in a language they can understand. My son especially has something of the same, a wild fellow deep inside. Yet a good and helpful boy, would never go in for a life of crime, no more than his father. I have never been a Nazi. Everyone should be allowed to mind his own business.

After military service, I began to construct my own pillow dummies from flour or sugar sacks. The first two were named after my then sweetheart, Ellen, (sugar sack, dark brown sugar), who was served by Hans (pea sack, yellow shelled peas, Hungarian) while I served my time as a soldier. I didn't appropriate the sacks with contents, however. For stuffing back then I used straw for her, chaff for him. It was only a one-shot expense, the stuffing could be used again and again, only the sacks had to be replaced. I tried to tack the first ones back together, but it bored me and besides they wore out easily, the canvas pulled at the seams.

I didn't try very hard to make the sacks resemble them. They consisted of a good-sized pea sack or mealsack for the body, a small lentil or raisin sack for the head, and then just some ends of packing twine for the arms and legs, just like in children's drawings. With charcoal and lipstick I smeared on eyes and mouth, sometimes also navel and breasts and that sort of thing. Then I hung them on a rope in a corner of the attic and started in on them. In the beginning I used mostly bread knives or wine bottles, after having knocked

the bottoms off on the edge of the kitchen sink, but later I
thought of beginning with sticking needles into them and
burning them with cigarettes in particularly exposed places. I had to give up the cigarette phase after I'd nearly
caused a fire and my landlady threatened to throw me out.
So I christened a sack in her name and switched over to
spraying nitric acid on her and the others, didn't aim at
anything in particular, simply splashed it and observed how
the acid ate in, kept on and on until by chance I hit the eyes
or the mouth or the sketched-in sexual parts. In between, I
spit or pissed on them, became formidable at the long-spit
and the long-piss. Finally I gave them the coup-de-grâce
with the .22 or bow. No one noticed anything, no one
complained or was injured, not even those I tortured or kil-
led, except that I became friendlier towards them, which
surprised them at first, but in several cases it resulted in my
becoming real friends with my victims and enemies. I became quite popular, never needed to say a bad word about
anyone, always had a friendly remark ready during the
afternoon rush and a disarming joke on my lips if anyone
annoyed me.

Soon I was promoted, became department head in South
Zealand, married locally, had local children, the business
thrived, customers flocked to me, I made new friends,
friends actually, only a few enemies, I was a contented person who built a fireplace and made peace with the dummies who lay idle in the attic. Still, they were living memories which lay in piles and collected mold, I had to go up
to them often and turn them over with a pitchfork, I laid
them by turns in the sun under the roof window to get
them completely dry, but the loft wasn't tight, fungus, mice
and decay devastated the straw, I had to change it twice a
year. Have you gotten a horse? They asked when I bought

one sack of straw after the other. I switched to foam rubber, it was quite expensive, but gave way in a more lifelike manner when you pressed on it. I could sit up there in my straw gallery for hours on cloudy afternoons. Once in a while for old enmity's sake I would puff a few pipe embers out over a bulging sack and watch how the embers tattooed curious black constellations.

»What are you doing up there?« my wife asked from the foot of the loft stairs.

»Thinking, smoking, relaxing,« I answered.

My wife is neither dumb, insensitive, nor markedly quarrelsome, on the contrary, she's practical and loving at the same time, she's from the country and with no sense for daydreams, meant well by me when she wanted the sacks out, conjugally unquiet with me if I remained sitting up there too long. »That deviltry is a haunt for mice, rats, cats, moths and wipers,« she affirmed loudly. Maybe it was true. The sacks shook themselves once in a while, there was squeaking in them, and twitchings. It could be either one thing or another. I remained fond of my wife and didn't neglect her in any way, so even though I saw no reason to relieve myself of the sacks, in the summer I hauled some of them out of the house for her sake and to keep the peace and gave them to my children to play with. They romped about emphatically with them, my girl hopped on them and rolled onto her back with a sack over her, my boy went at them with stick and sword, he picked it up quickly, had my temperment as far as sacks were concerned. An awful mess, said my wife about the chaff and foam rubber that abused the lawn. Let them have a good time, I answered, good, healthy children won't come to any harm from it.

»I want those pillows thrown out completely,« she said – – not combatively, rather pleadingly.

»We could convert the loft to something more sensible, a guest room, hobby room, clotheslines, whatever, the other is driving me crazy.«

So I went along with divesting myself of the dummies one by one, buried them down in remote dunes rather than lose my wife's reason. But I couldn't divest myself of the thought of them. I couldn't stand to look at, much less sit on, the small pretty embroidered pillows on the sofas, I became pillow-shy and spent still more time up in my now nearly empty loft, except for suitcases with old papers, chipped flowerpots no one had the heart to throw out completely, rusty basins and the like. I began to read books, the classics, in order to think better thoughts and maybe get an idea for the conversion of the loft, but the pillows drifted like clouds over the text:

»At times whilst I have meandered far out into the great All Pillow, where I have nothing but the brown heath about me and the blue Pillow above me, whilst I strayed far from Mankind and the Memorials of their Rustling here below, who are after all only Pillows . . .«

Then I took up going for long strenuous walks along the beach, but the terrain consisted of pillows, large, white pillows sailed over my head, I threw flintstones at them and they fell down onto sand pillows or heaped seaweed pillows, all the while the horizon perpetually afforded forest pillows, hill pillows, wave pillows.

After a while it was all I could do to entertain my customers in my previous jovial fashion, in addition a competing supermarket had sprung up, several of my steady customers deserted me before they'd finished paying their bills.

Furthermore, I had difficulty sleeping at night, my wife's breasts, shoulders, stomach, rear, which, by the way, are commendable, reminded me of my bygone pillows, while at the same time I was nearly suffocating in my own pillow. I continually made smaller and harder pillows, at last employed a box for kitchen matches. When that didn't help either, I saw no other alternative that to move to the loft, where I lay on the bare planks.

»Pull yourself together,« my wife wailed from the foot of the loft stairs. »The children are getting lower grades, we have no money for the milk bill, the man from the supermarket sits at the inn every day, winning the last of your customers at dice.«

»I'm not good at playing dice.«

Now my wife had to take care of both the shop and the children, so both suffered. In the main office they were greatly upset by my regression and were considering which was most propitious, a replacement or simply closing the branch.

»Why are you treating us this way?« my wife wept.

I didn't know what she meant, after all, I'd disposed of the pillows as she had wanted and laid down on this hard floor, which gave me splinters in my hands and made my limbs stiff, in order to forget them.

When the branch was closed, the supermarket bought out the business, the stock as well as the house here. The man from the supermarket had in mind to convert it to a warehouse. I decided then to keep lying in the loft until they carried me out. My wife had to take a job in the supermarket and moved there with the children. My son brought food to me, I tried to pump him about whether they were doing well, whether the man gave them chocolate, licorice, toys, whether he scolded them. He answered evasively, wouldn't say anything bad about anyone, wouldn't offend me, he was a genuine offshoot of his father, still I pressed him hard about whether mother was happy to be there, whether he had the impression she liked the man from the supermarket. Yes, yeah – – maybe – – that was all I got out of him. Whether there was anyone who had forbidden him to give me information? No, he said, but I couldn't tell whether he was lying, sometimes he resembled me almost too much. I shook him, weakened as I was it didn't amount to much, but enough so that he broke loose.

»Does he sometimes give you a pillow to wallop away at?«

He got pale and stood up.

»Well, he doesn't! I thought as much. Tell them for me that I'm coming to talk to him and mother about it. About everything. We have to get this settled. Tell them I've regained my strength.«

He hurried down the loft stairs before I'd finished speaking and I was alone with the streak of sun and the spiderwebs and the old gaping suitcases, the broken mirrors and the rusty basins. Probably he was dashing home now, to repeat my words, and then what wouldn't they think of? I had to act quickly. I sat up and ate the supermarket's oxtail soup, cold, felt my stomach and head grow heavy, lay down and fell asleep.

Something moved over in a corner. Something fat, dark, heavy, I wanted to rise on my butt to see if it was one of the sacks that had come back, but couldn't manage to lift my back from the floorboards. Cleared my throat and called: Is that you, Ellen – – how are you, it's been a long time – – aren't you glad that I didn't kill you, you were happy with Hans, is he with you? I looked, there was something that gathered behind a rafter, it was far into twilight, but it looked as though it could be an old acquaintance – – Come on out, Hans, I won't hurt you. I won't hurt anyone.

They didn't answer, but I couldn't hear my own voice, either, so either I've been deaf, or else I've been dead. Now the moonlight fell through the roof window and I could recognize more of the shapes.

»56, you old sadist, are you finally coming to apologize for pissing in my sodapop because I wouldn't drink beer? And the sergeant in person, is it all the injustices you've piled on me that makes you show up at last? It's been settled long ago, I wish you all the best, I wish no one harm, I am not at all a Nazi.«

They approach in the moonlight, and others bulge forward from behind him.

»Mom and Dad, I bear you no grudge for certain rash remarks, I'm a father myself, and my wife is herself a mother, we know how hard it can be −− first and foremost you made me very happy with those pillows −− come on in, you folks in the back, teacher Henriksen, and Mrs. Sørensen herself, my old landlady, it could have been much worse, we parted, I hope, as friends. I bless you all. Come and talk with me in my loneliness, stop standing there grumbling, can't you hear that I bless you? *I bless you all, each and every one, you dear old assholes!*

No, they don't hear, or I don't hear what they answer, but then I've got the excuse that I'm dead, anyway, then why do they stand there menacingly, they sway back and forth majestically with their coal eyes, coal navels, their powerless rope arms and legs, their rents and patches and their band-aids, I've blessed you, get yourselves out here now! Here I've lived to the end of my days, relatively, and then you roll in after the party's over, posthumously, I am dead, *dead*, Goddamn doornail *dead*! And I don't believe in hell, you can just as well leave at once, I want some peace, for Christ's sake!

Maybe I am mistaken. Even the dead can make mistakes, it's hard to see in the moonlight whether they're threatening me or just standing there gravely at my bed, perhaps will be good to me, it's impossible to tell from those coaldot eyes and stiff lipstick mouths, it can't be perceived from the drooping arm-ropes hanging down over me, unable to caress, strike, strangle or close my eyes. They lean in over me so I can no longer see the moonlight, they tumble onto me but I can't feel their weight because I'm dead, they press down around me, nuzzle their way under my loin, the hollows of my knees, lift me up, silently supporting me, my back, under my arms, under my knees, I'm lifted up into a bulging easy chair and float out through the roof window, over the trees, the hills, the henhouse.

Did I say anything, did it sound as if I said anything? Yes, at one point I tried to get it to sound as if I said: I can walk by myself. – – And, as if someone had heard me, which I didn't myself, they set me down and let me walk, that is, the bulging shapes supported me in such a way that my feet didn't touch the ground, and I tacitly agreed with it. Still I maintained periodic walking movements to indicate, at least, that I could walk if necessary. Their arm fringe and hair-twine tickled me in the ears and on the neck, but I ignored it and finally they set me down in front of the supermarket building.

The display was completely lit up in the middle of the night, illuminated pyramids of cans, columns of supermarket oxtail soup, peas, ham, hash from Fyn, peaches, no longer a single little toppled sack of dried plums or apricots. With the full use of my knuckles I knocked on the window of the living quarters.

It was a long time before a face appeared. A big square head with a jaw like a window frame and prophetic eyebrows.

»Isn't it a little late, not to say too late,« toned his organ voice. »You'd better let your wife sleep in peace, then she'll go home to you in the morning and make the necessary arrangements.«

»As you can see, I'm not alone,« I said and flung my arms about; my shirtsleeve was unbuttoned and flapped cape-like on my forearm. »We've come to take my wife and children home, we don't need to wake them at all, they'll be flown home as easy as pie.« He surveyed the host behind me and lifted his mail-slot smile slightly.

»Tomorrow they're coming to take you to a place where you can regain your health.«

I waved my fluttering armpendant in a friendly way.

»Allow me to explain myself more clearly: I don't need medical help, but my wife, without whom I couldn't be standing here today, but in any old place whatsoever. Furthermore, to say the least, I have recovered my health – – or if I may say it this way: health has come to me.«

In answer came a big burst sausage into view through his mail-slot mouth and spit the leftover food (canned food, very gristly) at me, whereupon he slammed the window shut. I understood him very well, wished him no harm, didn't even once think about making a pillow-dummy of him, had angels enough around me, but felt compelled to give the signal to storm the building. Without shedding blood or foam rubber! sounded my command.

I won't dwell on the consequent rumbling in the chimneys, the banging of doors and windows, the din behind cupboards and panels, I retreated discreetly and began to walk homeward across the hills.

My wife rushed out in pajamas and hair curlers.

»Go home,« she screamed. »Stop plaguing us, go home now!«

I turned and stroked her gently on the curlers, which only upset her all the more, and said:

»You can see very well that I am on my way home.«

»You've always wrapped yourself up in your cowardly self-pity!« she blubbered and held my flapping arms.

»My self-pity I've kept to myself,« I said, and unloosened her hair curlers, »is that wrong?«

»You should have shared it with us rather than your infamous dummies, it would have been much better if you had bawled me out, walloped me when you were mad at someone else.«

»Before you said that I should leave you alone, now even *that's* wrong. There where my self-pity stops, your compassion begins, a first-rate feeling, but it doesn't really go with supermarket.«

I broke loose from her and began to walk quickly down the meadow path to our beach house. I felt light and elastic as if I hadn't lain for weeks in the hard loft.

»I'm sorry I took your pillows from you,« she screamed from behind.

I turned around and saw her lying flat on her face in the path with her hair over her arms. Farther down appeared the painted sacks from the supermarket buildings, fatigued from their havoc, didn't exactly hover, supported themselves, breathless, against each other, and stumbled over stones and tufts of grass on their wobbly ribbon-legs.

»You're wrong,« I shouted and ran back to her, »on the contrary, you've saddled me with them for real!«

I lifted her up and tried to run with her. I could really feel now that I wasn't in very good shape. Just like my pursuers I stumbled over meadow tufts, fragments of stone and hedgehogs, lost valuable time besides by looking back and went weak in the knees at the sight: the row of sacks had spread out, the moon shone on the unbleached Hessian with coal and lipstick inscriptions, they swayed foward shoulder to shoulder on their daddy-longlegs in a half-circle formation in order to cut us off.

I tottered forward again, but couldn't straighten my legs out, needed a running start.

Then my wife moaned: »Idiot!«

At once I flew home effortlessly with her in my arms, just managed to slam the door on Hans at the last second, his right arm-twine got caught, I pulled it and tore it loose without effort, it had only been attached with sewing thread in the first place.

»What now,« my wife complained, lying in a triangular position on the straw mat.

»None of them can get in without my knowing it.«

»What about the children?«

I had to phone down to the terror-stricken supermarket.

»The children are safe and sound under their beds, but where is your wife? She responded to all my shouts and suggestions with pillows, the apartment is littered with feathers, all the cans in the store are knocked over and dented, ketchup bottles emptied out on the walls and counters, cookies, flowerseeds, and pudding mix spread everywhere, the cash register is rung up wrong . . .«

The sacks stood on each other's backs and pushed their lifeless faces against the window in order to get in.

»You've lost your mind,« my wife wept, »don't you realize it? They're coming tomorrow to get you, we've arranged the time!«

She looked for her curlers.

»They're already out there now,« I said. »A snap of the fingers from me, and they'll be all over us as ordered.«

»Don't snap,« she pleaded.

The telephone croaked again on the little teak table: »The dog has run away, the neighbors are complaining, the oranges are over-ripe, the bananas unripe, the raisins too dry, the flour too damp, the beer labels are crooked, aren't you ashamed . . .«

»I'll come in tomorrow and put it in order, I'm inclined to go into business with you, on certain conditions. I know the customers, not least of all those from the outlying districts . . .«

»Never!« came the scream from the receiver, »Never on your life! From the outlying districs they come and complain about cornflakes and oatmeal, shampoo, chocolate liqueur . . .«

»I'll come get the children in the morning,« I said firmly, »so you may have until then to decide whether you want me for a partner or a competitor. Confidentially, I'm holding all the cards,« (I glanced at my wife, who lay on the bed talking wildly while she tried to set in thread spools for curlers).

»If they are coming for me tomorrow,« I said, slamming down the receiver, »you'll have to sign on the dotted line that you are my guardian or keeper or private nurse or whatever it's called. Otherwise we'll never get to have the children.«

I pulled off her dress, threw the thread spools on the floor and took hold of her curved, resilient thigh, but she doubled up so that she got her long hair in her mouth. Who knows what he had done to her. But it will be a big day tomorrow, a remarkable day. We'll handle it all right, but how?

Wake up, Sophie, I wish no one any harm, I've never been a Nazi, and our children are far from criminals, I'm a good father, an honest employer, a suitable husband, my friend's friend, and my enemies', I have blessed you all for many hours, so let me go! Get away from the windows, we will have a busy day tomorrow, a big day, a remarkable day, but Rome as you know wasn't built in ... we have to get some sleep, too ... in turns ... wake up, Sophie, Rome wasn't built in one day, can you hear me, it definitely wasn't ... tomorrow I have to explain it all to the kids in a language they can understand ... wake up now, Sophie, before I fall asleep ...